I0720180

By Kaylea Prime

By Kaylea Prime

Tears of Flame

<u>Novels</u>
A Spark From Embers

<u>Novellas</u>
A Ballad of Hate and Hope

KAYLEA
PRIME

A BALLAD OF HATE AND HOPE

A TEARS OF FLAME NOVELLA

This book is a work of fiction. Any references to historical events, real people, or real places are used fictitiously. Other names, characters, places, and events are products of the author's imagination, and any resemblance to actual events, locales, organizations, or persons, living or dead, is entirely coincidental.

Copyright © 2023 by Kaylea Prime

All rights reserved.

No part of this publication may be reproduced, distributed, or transmitted in any form or by any means, including photocopying, recording, or other electronic or mechanical methods, without the prior written permission of the copyright owner, except for the use of quotations in a book review. For more information or permission requests, contact Storms & Starscapes Publishing at info@kayleaprime.com. Thank you for your support of the author's rights.

Cover design by Miblart

Interior Design by Kaylea Prime

First edition: October 2023

ISBN 978-1-7380885-0-8 (paperback)

ISBN 978-1-7380885-1-5 (ebook)

www.kayleaprime.com

For Bethany

Contents

One

Of all the stories vying for attention in Nensola's head, stories of hope were the loudest.

Not love, as she had once naively assumed.

Not hate, as she had feared, though those had the sharpest sting.

But simple, unassuming hope.

Gripping the sea-slick black rock with pruned fingers, Nensola peered at the man bobbing in the reef and reminded her pounding heart of hope's prevalence in the stories she recounted as a Storyteller.

Dawn's first light had stretched to paint the clouds' underbellies ruby when he had arrived, materializing suddenly in a wave's surf. Spluttering and choking on the foam, he had tumbled beneath the wave's strong, pummeling arms before breaking free into the calmer waters of the transparent turquoise reef. Now he treaded water with practised ease, long arms sculling like a sea turtle's flippers, dipping his face intermittently underwater to examine the peach coral. She hoped his sudden arrival did not mean trouble, but her bruised heart warned against such optimism.

Strange men materializing on Lothilya's shores at odd hours rarely meant anything good.

Yet he had arrived alone, with no ship. No hardened, grim purpose thinned his lips or flashed in his eyes. His slackened lips quirked at one corner, the ghost of a smile haunting a face open in surprised wonder. He seemed in no hurry, content to wiggle his fingers at the red-gold phoenixfish darting around his legs and torso curiously like dancing beams of the sunrise.

Nensola forced the breath hitched against the roof of her mouth to release between her clenched teeth, grateful the lapping water masked the uneven hiss.

It should take nothing to hope this human, with his sun-bronzed tawny skin and hair like curls of cloves, meant no harm. To assume his innocence.

And yet it took everything.

Hope is never unassuming.

Her sister Setamíel's words from seven years ago still lanced Nensola's mind like the sharp spear her sister carried these days, weighted with despair from the sticky, gummed lips of a thir-teen-year-old Lantíe whose hope had drained with the last of her salty tears.

"Hope assumes there is good in people," Setamíel had rasped, choking on dry sobs. "Hope assumes there is a guiding moral compass. That people will have beliefs and stand up for them. That they will fight for what they love."

Setamíel's voice had wavered, splintering like a cracked *phylorax* shell bereft of a shimmering orb. "But there is no map to kindness. There is only greed, and self-preservation. People don't care for anyone but themselves."

"Mom cared," ten-year-old Nensola had said, her voice meek, small even to her own ears. "Mom always said there was no hate stronger than hope."

"Mom was *wrong*!" Setamíel had screamed. "Hate will always be stronger than hope."

Nensola had recoiled at her sister's hardened words, ears ringing as though slapped.

And yet as she had slammed open the door and stumbled to the beach, throat burning and hands shaking, her mother's voice had whispered in her ear. Even now, seven years later, Nensola questioned whether the words wrapping her in comfort that night had been a memory's echo breathed to life or a manifestation of her gift as a Storyteller.

Hope has no beginning, and no end. Her mother's voice rolled across the sun-dappled waves again now, rising and falling like the rumbling, rushing rhythm of expanding lungs.

Nensola wanted to hope. She craved the security of hope's promise. The warm contentment stories of past hopes embraced her with when she recalled them in song.

But the concept of hope remained elusive. When she relayed stories of hope so strong it felled armies and throned queens, she tried to snatch the feeling for herself, bottle it like a secret message delivered on the waves. But she could never find a cork. Hope just leaked back out as soon as it poured in.

She watched the man tilt his head back and lift his torso to the deep burnt-orange sky, floating with limbs splayed wide like a palm frond.

Slowly she climbed the rest of the way down the rock, never taking her eyes off the man, until she felt the grainy crunch of sand between her bare toes. Her creamy white antlers caught on the low-hanging branch of a tree overshadowing the rock, and she shook her head slightly to free them.

Voices clamoured in her head, images of blood mingled with seafoam and jagged edges of broken ship planks surfacing in her mind, but she pushed them aside.

When she was a child, the voices had swelled in her mind, bleeding together in a cacophony of desperate shrieks and layered whispers. Pressure would build until she screamed, pressing small hands to her pointed ears.

Cradling up her taut body curled against the onslaught of stories roiling in her head like a storm, her mother would rush her out to the stream behind their home and stick her hand in the water, murmuring sweet assurances against the curls of her teal-threaded black hair.

Nensola would press her ear against her mother's chest, listening to the steady thrum of her heart. Breathing in her scent of brine and pomelo fruit. Letting the cool water slip between her fingers, relaxing her limbs, unfurling her violet-tipped, bronze-feathered wings.

Slowly the voices would quiet, mute to a steady stream, babbling gently through her mind like a river sliding over rocks.

Stories that prodded without clamouring.

"That's it, Nensola, that's it," her mother would croon, placing her hand on the back of her daughter's, the one still plunged in the stream. "Feed the excess from your mind to the stream. Let the water siphon the voices, filter the stories. Allow yourself to listen, instead of blocking them out."

Her mother taught her how to tame the tidal wave of voices surging in the sudden story storms. How to listen.

Eventually, she had learned the cadences of the voices. The melodies of sorrows and triumphs, of loves and losses, of discoveries and wonders, of horrors and pains. She had interpreted the images blooming in her head, unfolding like the wings of a butterfly as it sheds its chrysalis.

And she had learned every story had a theme.

A lesson to be learned, an observation about life. A feeling to spread across the soul like sticky molasses, the sweet or bitter taste lingering long after the story ends.

A tone that could be measured by sound.

Love was a murmur, a warm whisper in her ear.

Hate was a curse, barbed and sharp, and hurled with venom.

But hope was a shout, loud and clear, and impossible to ignore.

When stories of hope beckoned to Nensola, they demanded to be heard.

She couldn't ignore them, even if all her other senses were consumed by anger or terror.

Even when her heart was torn to shreds like brittle parchment. When her mother had died and it had felt like it would never mend.

Hope still spoke louder than grief.

Her sister would say hope was a privilege. A luxury for mortals whose existence was not feared by half of Arwé for a past they couldn't control. A luxury for a race whose dark history did not include evolving from perytons, winged deer known for preying on human souls from parallel worlds. A luxury for beings who did not continue to be associated with forbidden Celestial magic.

Beings born with no pre-existing prejudices could afford hope.

But not the Lantíé.

Many of the hopeful stories she recalled *were* about mortals and other races.

But not all.

The Lantíé had stories of hope too.

And no matter what Setamíel said, Nensola needed those stories. She needed to know that the dark shadows creeping across the story images in her mind when she struggled to control the voices were not shadows of past peryton victims—that the black, murky waters of her heart did not foreshadow future victims.

Pressing her pruned fingers against her thumb, she took a tentative step toward the man.

She could lead with hope or barricade it behind steel walls, like Setamíel.

White sand shifted beneath her feet, but her steps were steady.

She flexed her long, powerful wings and felt the feathers ruffle in the ocean breeze.

The man flailed his arms and bolted upright, sending droplets skittering across the water like skipping stones. His eyes settled on Nensola standing at the water's edge, wavelets lapping across her toes, and widened.

Nensola's heart skipped like the water droplets, rippling throughout her body, but she couldn't tell if the erratic beats stuttered in fear or anticipation.

With a few powerful strokes, he reached shallower waters and walked toward her.

When he drew closer, she could see his wide eyes held no fear. They glinted with ... could that be ... awe?

Pausing with the water still eddying around his shins, he lifted a lean arm past narrower shoulders and a more rounded jaw than she had at first thought, and raked a hand through his sopping hair awkwardly. Not a man but a boy, maybe around her seventeen years.

Filling her lungs like the swell of a wave, bracing for the inevitable tumble after her words broke upon his ears, she unfurled her fingers and extended her palms in greeting.

"*Ekalé.*"

Two

Torrential rain pelted Kit's cheeks, stinging his raw skin and streaming down his jawline to drip off his chin. Fierce wind billowed the sails and lashed the rigging, rocking the ship in the waves' arms like a parent desperate to hush their inconsolable infant. The ship's hull creaked and groaned in defiance, heard even over the roar of smashing storm-swollen waves.

"Secure the stays!" barked a gruff voice from the helm.

Kit rushed to obey his father's orders without looking at him. A few crewmen joined him at the mainmast, and together they tugged and hauled on the lines until they were taut and secure.

"Kit!" his father bellowed when the ship's sway became a little less vigorous.

Squinting through watery eyes, Kit spotted his father silhouetted against the golden glow spilling through the open doorway of the captain's quarters, gesturing for his son to join him. Tantalizing though the warm lamplight's invitation was, Kit hesitated. He glanced around the deck, but the crew still busied themselves with steadying the ship, unaware of or unconcerned by the captain's obvious favouritism.

Hunching his shoulders and shoving hands bleached clammy white from the rain into his breeches' pockets, pooled with water, Kit shuffled over to the stern cabin and entered first.

An involuntary sigh escaped his lips as he sank into a rickety chair opposite his father's desk. He peeled his drenched white linen shirt from his chest and reached for his leather boots to empty them of the water sloshing around the ankles of his wool stockings, but his father held up a staying hand.

"You empty that smelly sea slime in my cabin, and you'll be swabbing up sea sick and food scum for a week," he growled.

Kit returned his boot to the scrubbed cabin deck with an unpleasant squelch.

Removing his dripping, rain-soaked tricorn hat, Captain Firth peered at Kit with beady, midnight-blue eyes set above a high-bridged nose. Candlelight flickered over his freckled sandy skin, deepening the shadows staining the sagging circles beneath his eyes and snagging on the lines of his wrinkles.

"This storm's only getting worse," Captain Firth stated, watching for Kit's reaction. "If we don't decide soon, we'll all be lost to a watery grave. Sometimes no choice can be worse than the wrong choice."

Kit flinched. The mistake alluded to had been his father's, not Kit's, but the words still grated on his scabbed heart, reopening wounds still too fresh to have fully healed.

"Sorry, son," muttered his father. "I don't mean to upset you. I just want you to learn from my mistakes."

"I know," mumbled Kit, wiping an errant raindrop from the tip of his nose. His gaze shifted to the contraption on the desk between them, drawn to its metallic whirring like a bee drawn to nectar. "I *have* been thinking about our options. But it's a bit difficult when bartering with local, respectable sailors might lead to you being turned over to the Royal Navy in Port Royal, and presenting the device to the Board of Longitude in England yourself to claim the prize directly would result in a definite hanging. I want you to be safe."

"Aye, I suppose we're caught between the devil and the deep sea," his father lamented.

"A pirate's favourite place to be," rhymed Kit cheekily.

Captain Firth snorted and winked at his son. "Isn't that the truth of it!"

Rubbing the back of his neck, his father looked out at the bruised twilight sky, pewter clouds bloated with the promise of more rain. "We do need to make a decision, though, whether it benefits me personally or not," he continued. "I won't be so bold as to claim I'm a selfless pirate—the very concept is a damn oxymoron—but there is the crew to think about. We haven't got unlimited supplies. We need the money. The crew might even mutiny if we don't satiate their appetites soon. And right now, this devil-cursed longitude device is the only leverage we have."

"There is a third option," said Kit, bracing for the heat of his father's inevitable anger, but needing to revisit the idea again. "We could barter with another pirate. We'd get a lower price, but at least we'd get *something*."

Captain Firth bristled, hand instinctively darting to the pistol resting at his waist. Kit didn't even blink, knowing the gesture was not to threaten him but to protect him.

"*No pirates,*" his father spat, his words sharpened to a knife's edge. "I don't trust any of those cowardly bilge rats to cut a fair deal, and what's more, they're likely as not to blast us to smithereens as soon as we hand the damn contraption over. I'm not risking the lives of the whole crew when I could just risk my life. I'm not risking *your* life like that. Yours is far more precious than mine, lad. Your mother would have tossed me overboard herself."

"She wouldn't thank you for leaving me parentless either," muttered Kit.

"You watch your tongue, boy," Captain Firth growled in warning. He paced the cabin deck, boots clunking and buckles jingling with every step. "I may not always do right by you, but I've done my best to see to it your future is taken care of while still avenging your mother. I once trusted where I shouldn't have trusted, and it cost me everything. I won't make the same mistake again, not when it means losing the only thing I care about in this godforsaken world."

"And you're so sure Mother would have wanted to be avenged?" Kit countered, picking at a splinter on the wooden desk to distract himself from the sudden heat scorching his stomach and rising to his chest. "The British invaded Gibraltar, killed the love of her life right in front of her, forcing us to flee our home—"

"You don't have to remind me or convince me of the atrocities my people committed, son," Captain Firth interrupted, pausing his pacing to regard Kit with shifting, awkward eyes. "I'm aware your mother had every right to loathe the British. To loathe me at first too. No doubt she would have avenged your father herself if she could have without putting you in danger. I ... I know Esperanza never loved me as she loved Eduardo. I knew she never would when I married her. She *told* me she never would."

Kit's father shook his head slightly, a small, bemused smile twitching at the corners of his lips and pride shining in his eyes—an almost possessive pride Kit wasn't sure his father had earned. "Your mother was a passionate woman. She loved fiercely; she loathed fiercely; she protected her past fiercely; and she made bold choices from the heart without regret."

Squeezing his eyes shut, Kit pinched the skin between his eyebrows with both hands. Why was he picking a fight with his father? He knew Captain Firth had loved his mother and loved him, yet he couldn't stop the heat burning his eyes, couldn't bite his tongue hard enough to stop the words from lashing out.

"Her own people shunned her when she married you to secure a future for me. They called her a traitor for daring to see a British person as anything but a heartless conqueror. She had to witness her son shed his heritage like a snake sheds old skin." Kit's voice rose with each accusation he rattled off, anger's heat scalding his tongue, but he wouldn't be diverted from the truth he *needed* to speak. "She carried the burden of past and future alone while we set sail on expeditions for the empire that had crushed her dreams. The British cost *her* everything, not you. She didn't even die by their hands; she died of smallpox. I don't think you became a pirate to avenge Mom. I think you did it to avenge your own wounded pride."

Kit watched the words pepper his father's heart like bullets.

Captain Firth's slackened lips parted, but no sound shattered his shocked silence.

At first.

"Christopher Firth, how *dare* you—"

"*Don't* full-name me with my English name like that!" shouted Kit, pounding his fists against the table as he leapt to his feet. The rising heat clawed at his throat and burned his cheeks. He tried to swallow, to soothe it with his saliva, but his voice still rasped and broke when he hurled his next words at his stepfather. "I'm not Christopher Firth, but thanks to you, I'm no longer Pedro Aguado either. I don't fit in with the English, and I don't feel at home with the Spanish. I am just Kit. Reduced to a nickname, a name for someone with no identity. Lost between cultures, adrift at sea with no anchor or ropes. Nothing to tie me to shore. Did it ever occur to you that you're the only thing *I* have left?"

Candlelight flickered across his father's face, but the dancing light couldn't mask the flinch in Captain Firth's eyes. He blinked rapidly, as though trying to clear spotty vision after a slap. After clearing his throat, he looked down at his boots and grunted, "I'm honoured to be your anchor, son. Of course I don't want you to lose that. But you're my anchor too. And without this money, we will both be adrift. We may never find our way back. I … I'll think on it tonight, and let you know my decision in the morning."

Kit recognized the dismissal.

With one last glance at the longitude device, Kit trudged out of the cabin, water sloshing in his boots with every step.

But even the torrential rain hammering his shoulders as he rejoined the crew couldn't distract him from his father's plight over the enigmatic longitude device.

Despite the swell of anger at his father's insistence that his obsession with revenge was a selfless act, Kit knew Captain Firth was a good man. And a good father. He had encouraged Kit to speak of his biological father, Eduardo, to keep his memory alive. Kit would always be grateful to his stepfather for that.

He couldn't let his father die. It was true he had no anchor or ropes to tie him to a home, but his father was his guiding star, the heading his compass could always point to. With his father, he could still chart a course through life, maybe even navigate to a real home one day. Without him, he would be truly lost.

Glancing back at the orange glow in the windows of the captain's cabin, Kit gritted his teeth and squared his shoulders.

Words were not Captain Firth's preferred form of currency.

So Kit would barter with a currency he understood far better: action.

Tiptoeing across the rough wooden deck on his bare feet, Kit wended his way through sleeping pirates sprawled on shabby cots and threadbare hammocks, avoiding the creaky boards with practised steps. The hull swayed like a pendulum, threatening to destabilize Kit's careful creeping toward the ladder ascending to the upper deck. A violent lurch forced him to stumble and trip over his feet. He threw out his hands and wrapped his fingers around a rung to steady his shaking knees.

A quick glance around the lower deck assured him no one had stirred at his stumbling. Releasing a slow breath through his clenched teeth, Kit slowly began to climb the ladder.

Usually Kit's sea legs were strong, but this storm raged harder than any he'd experienced before. Captain Firth had ordered the crew to get some sleep earlier when the storm had calmed a bit, but it must have worsened recently if the pirate on watch hadn't woken them up to deal with it yet. When Kit's head crested the hatch's opening to the upper deck and jagged veins of lightning greeted him against the storm-blackened sky, he swallowed hard and considered trying to steal the longitude device tomorrow night instead.

But no. It had to be tonight. His father had promised he'd share his decision in the morning, and his word held more value than gold. A decision meant a heading, and Captain Firth would waste no time setting sail immediately after announcing the new heading to his crew.

Kit glanced at the helm, but the pirate on watch was slumped against the pedestal, an open bottle of whisky in one hand. He must have been trying to stay warm and had too much, but it would cost him his job. Waking him could wait until after Kit had stolen the contraption. Nothing stirred in the darkness framed behind the mullioned windows of the captain's cabin. The candles had been snuffed out.

Kit took a deep breath, then hoisted himself onto the deck and stole surreptitiously toward the cabin.

Lightning flashed, illuminating the cabin's worn doorknob. Kit seized it and froze, not daring to even breathe while he counted in his head.

One ... two ... three ... fou—

BOOM!

Thunder clapped, so loud Kit's ears rang. He turned the rickety doorknob, opening the creaky cabin door under the guise of the thunder's resounding rumbles. Before the reverberations faded, Kit had clicked the door shut again.

Peering at the shifting shadows blotting the cabin's corners, Kit could just make out the ripples of the heavy velvet curtain hiding his father's narrow berth, built into an alcove behind the desk. Subtle snores rolled out from behind the curtain in rhythm with the crashing waves outside. Kit's chest loosened a little, but he remained wary. His father's light-sleeping habit could still alert him to Kit's presence at the slightest noise.

He padded across the deck to the desk, pressing his feet as lightly as possible and extending his hands in front of him so he wouldn't bump into anything. When his fingers brushed the rough edge of the desk, he started scuttling them across the surface like a spider, trying to feel for the device.

Lightning branched across the sky outside, briefly illuminating the cabin's interior through the window.

Kit's heart slammed against his rib cage like a prisoner desperate to avoid the gallows, but he didn't waste the opportunity. He grabbed the longitude device while the flash of light lingered, then stuffed it under the sash at his waist. He backed toward the door as quickly and quietly as he could, never taking his eyes off the curtain hiding his father. With each step, he counted.

One ... two ... thr—

Thunder roared before he could finish the three in his head.

Panicking, Kit flew to the door, desperate to open it while the thunder still masked its creaking. He fumbled with the doorknob and pushed it open.

Captain Firth snorted and coughed.

Ears ringing, heart pounding, mouth dry, Kit stepped out into the sudden deluge of rain and clicked the cabin door shut behind him.

Wind slapped his face and whipped his shirt, pummeling his side with heavy fists until he staggered sideways. Planting his feet further apart and bending his knees against the gale's force, he squinted through the downpour.

The storm rapidly worsened. Layers of black thunderclouds quilted the sky. Bolts of lightning now leapt from several different focal points, and the waves beating against the hull bulged so high they splashed across the deck, drenching Kit's bare feet.

He should wake his father.

He *couldn't* wake his father. Captain Firth would notice the longitude device's absence immediately. Kit would have to give it back, and his father would never trust him again.

But if he didn't wake him, trying to save his father would be a moot point. The whole ship could keel over, and they'd perish at sea.

Kit raked fingers through his hair and pulled. His frustrated curse was lost to another thunderclap as he turned to wake his father—and found him standing two inches from his face.

The blood rushing to Kit's ears from his racing heart deafened the storm's cacophony.

"Where is it, boy?" Captain Firth hissed.

Kit swallowed hard. "Where's what?"

"Don't play with me, son. I have no patience for bilge-sucking traitors. Hand it over, or you'll be spending the entire journey in the brig. Savvy?"

Footsteps thudded across the deck, crew members racing from the ladder to their stations to get the rocking ship under control. Kit would bet his last coin the lower deck had started flooding, and this had woken the rest of the crew.

"The storm ... I was just coming to wake you ..." Kit fumbled, taking a step back.

"Do you think I'm stupid?" his father demanded, voice starting to rise.

"No, of course not. I—"

"Captain!" bellowed a voice from the crow's nest above. "Maelstrom!"

Both Captain Firth and Kit looked up to see the pirate clinging to the rail of the crow's nest with one hand and pointing toward the starboard side with the other. Though Kit couldn't see his face clearly through the slanting rain, the man's voice broke in terror.

Kit and his father looked at each other, an unspoken agreement to pause their argument passing between them.

Reaching the starboard side first, Kit felt his stomach lurch, and he gripped the railing *hard*.

"Well, shit," his father whispered beside him.

Powerful, foam-lipped eddies swirled in a huge whirlpool less than a dozen feet away. The midnight-blue sea spiraled down the vortex to the black depths of the ocean.

"Hard to port!" his father shouted at the crew, leaping into action. He sprinted to take the helm.

But Kit couldn't move.

Waves battered against the hull, pushing the ship toward the maelstrom. All around him pirates shouted themselves hoarse in panic, heaving and pulling and steering with all their might.

But Kit couldn't tear his eyes away from the hypnotic swirls of the maelstrom's current. They pulled him in. A force stronger than the moon's pull on the tide, more unrelenting than the arms of a mother protecting her baby.

Slowly the maelstrom reeled them in.

Kit leaned over the railing and stared into the eye of the storm.

The ship leaned with him.

The keel lifted out of the water. The ship teetered on the brink of the maelstrom, balanced for a brief second at an impossible angle.

A second too long.

Kit pitched over the side.

"*Kit!*"

His father's terrified scream echoed in his ears as he plunged, back first, into the maelstrom.

Walls of water towered over him, blocking his view of the shrinking ship and stormy sky. He hit the water with a smack and was yanked under, pulled in faster, tighter circles. The weight of the ocean crushed him, pinning him down. He flailed, trying to pull his head out of the water enough to breathe, but the vortex sucked him mercilessly down.

Spluttering and choking, lungs filling with water and vision blurring, Kit glimpsed a distorted, glassy circle beneath him, like the filmy sheen of a giant bubble, before black spots crowded his vision.

He floated in darkness, cradled in its tender embrace.

His lungs drained. Pain ceased.

If this was death, it was peaceful. Gentle.

Had anything in life ever been this gentle?

Was this the mortality humanity feared?

Maybe he should not have dreaded his father's death after all.

Light bloomed before him like a flower unfolding its petals.

Soft at first but growing brighter. And bluer.

Bluer?

This wasn't death. It was water. He still floated in the ocean.

Panic raked his lungs, and he kicked wildly without knowing which way was up. A few powerful strokes of his arms later, his head broke the surface. He sucked huge swallows of air in gasps. His lungs burned. Coughs clawed past his raw throat, and salty bile spilled out of his mouth. Kit caught a glimpse of ruby-dappled clouds before a wall of water rushed toward him.

"You have *got* to be kidding me!" he shouted as the wave crested above him. It slammed him back below the surface. Tumbling beneath the wave like a boulder rolling down a hill, Kit smacked his knee against a rock, and then he shot out of the wave's current like a cannonball.

Dazed, Kit opened his eyes to find the surface.

Turquoise water surrounded him, calm and dappled with a blood orange light shining above his ear. Kit kicked to the surface. For a few minutes after his lungs found oxygen, all he could concentrate on was treading water and regulating his breathing. When his breathing steadied to a normal pace and his head stopped swimming, he remembered the longitude device. Fumbling at his waist, he felt a hard square lump under his sash and exhaled in relief. Somehow the device had survived the maelstrom.

Taking a deep, steadying breath, he focused on his surroundings.

He bobbed in the calm, transparent waters of a reef more vibrant and colourful than he remembered the reefs of Grenada being. Fuchsia, violet, and bright orange coral decorated the ocean floor's white sand, and exotic fish in a variety of colours and patterns weaved between the coral.

When he swivelled toward the shore, Kit's jaw dropped.

A village bordered the white sand beach on the near side of what appeared to be a peninsula. Strange driftwood-and-clay houses with roofs thatched with palm fronds and seaweed sidled up to the sand. Palm trees mingled with birch, ash, and elm trees. Colourful hammocks swung between their trunks, and strings of shells and shiny sea gems dangled from their branches, tinkling in a slight breeze. Docks of woven grass, reeds, and tree bark supported by log pillars stretched out over the reef in places, and fishing nets had been cast out from many of them.

No ships dotted the horizon. No trace of his father or his crewmates. Or the maelstrom. This was not the same ocean he had almost drowned in.

Where am I?

He pushed the question from his mind and floated on his back, resting his weary legs and gazing up at the sun-painted clouds. Right now, the answer didn't seem important. He was alive. And this place was wondrous.

Concern for his father couldn't be pushed away for long, though. Had he survived the maelstrom? Kit's chest ached as he imagined his father alive but assuming his son was dead. If Kit really was his anchor ... he shuddered to think what his father would become when fully adrift.

A soft *whoosh* whistled past his ear like the echo of a gale, and his torso sank. Startled, he flailed his arms and turned toward the sound.

Someone stood on the white sandy beach.

Someone with *wings.*

Mesmerized, Kit swam toward her, only stopping to walk when his feet could touch the sand. Her seafoam-green eyes glinted with guarded determination and matched her metallic dress of the same colour. White deer-like antlers sprouted from teal-threaded black hair, and her deep black skin had a silvery tinge like moonlight glinting off a gently flowing midnight river. The violet-tipped bronze feathers ruffled as she shifted her wings.

Words caught in his throat, so he raked a hand through his sopping hair.

She uncurled the fingers of both hands and held them in front of her.

"*Ekalé*," she said. Her melodious voice struck a chord in his soul, reminding him of the lilting notes in his mother's musical Spanish.

"Uh ... hello," Kit said, sliding his jaw to the side awkwardly. "Or ... *hola*?"

She looked at him blankly.

Undeterred, Kit smiled and extended his hands, palms up, the way she had.

"*Ekalé*," he greeted her, testing the word on his tongue.

Her smile glowed brighter than the piercing rays of the sun rising above the trees behind her. Kit's stomach swooped, his heart stuttering an erratic beat.

Slowly his anchor began to lower.

Three

One year later

Nensola trailed her fingers through the gently gurgling stream carving a path through the woods bordering the Ataní palace, dividing the flow of water like she divided the flow of stories in her mind. Barricading certain themes, filtering the superfluous, redirecting character arcs, and creating confused eddies that swirled storylines together and churned out new trajectories.

Her fingers danced through the water, deftly working the currents like an Armindí Weaver threading strands of Earth magic through their clothing. Siphoning the tidal wave of stories like her mother had taught her.

But inside, panic still choked her thoughts. It squeezed her chest, bubbling up her neck and blurring her vision, tingling down to her numb fingertips. The cool water tempered the heat of too many stories crowding her mind. Overwhelming her. Taking control.

She could still see the shadows hovering around the edges of the story she had been singing. The black tendrils creeping across her story of resilience, tainting the hero's conviction with doubt and darkness. Hollowing out her own heart, filling it with the bleak emptiness of despair.

Nensola hated performing in the palace. Crowds ignited the stories in her head, smothering her own thoughts with narratives inspired by their emotions. The sea of faces blurred. The judging, impatient eyes of the nobles bored into her skull. Whispers of her young age, her inexperience, her combination of wings and antlers, which marked her as an anomaly even among the Lantíé, her own kind. Control became a tenuous string she clung to by one fraying thread. Most of the time, she could keep the shadows at bay and fight the rising panic down enough to finish her song. But not always. Often she would have to flee from the Hall of Stories, her long wings snagging on hems as she pushed through the crowd to the palace grounds.

But Lord Eberon and Lady Leilaní always asked her to return, and she could not refuse them. Despite her eccentricities, she was the best Storyteller in Lothilya, and they didn't let her forget it.

No one ever let her forget.

Breathing deeply through her nose, Nensola watched the silver sheen of a cloudy afternoon snag the stream's ripples, dappling the dark water with light. Not even clouds could stop the sun from bringing light to dark places. So why were Nensola's clouds so opaque? When would the hope her mother always promised shine through?

She was so tired of hiding from her own thoughts. From the dark shadows that stained her stories and mind. For once, it would be nice to see the fear in the other Carmellian races' eyes when they saw her wings and antlers and not wonder if it was justified—if she was, in fact, a monster.

A song came to her, clear and strong, rising above the others she had muted. With her hand in the water, she closed her eyes and embraced the image of a woman with blue skin and kelp wings. Pumping powerfully like giant sea turtle flippers, they propelled her through the ocean and up to the shadow of a ship passing above. When her head broke the surface, the storm kelpie opened her mouth to challenge the sailors to a poetry battle in exchange for passing through the waters of her home—but the words stuck in her throat.

An Armindí woman stood at the prow, raven hair streaked with bands of white framing her face. She stared steadily at the storm kelpie through black onyx eyes, unperturbed by her sudden appearance. The corner of her thin lips quirked a challenge in more ways than one.

Singing softly to herself, Nensola fit words to the images as they shifted in her mind.

Fingers intertwined, the Armindí woman and storm kelpie splashed and swam in the shallows of a reef, basking in the intoxicating glow of sunlight and laughter.

"Oní delt äns mié fi laurel."

Moonlight filtered through the tapered tips of the birch leaves shading the tree they perched in. The shadows between moonbeams masked the storm kelpie's smile as she tucked the Armindí's hair behind her ear and whispered something.

"Duko é ettë on car anu sula."

The Armindí tipped the storm kelpie's chin up a little and stole a kiss. Chuckling softly, she leapt to her feet, balancing on a branch, and jumped into the air. She tucked her body in for a flip, and when she uncurled, she had shape-shifted. Wings as wide as a young dragon's, ebony feathers blotting out the moon, sharp talons flexing. A white stripe starting above each eye and trailing out across each wing to the tip. The Armindí had transformed into a lightning bird.

"Ono mié let ä ukra."

The Armindí flew below heavy pewter clouds in her lightning bird form, summoning bolts of lightning and booms of thunder with each beat of her wings. In the dark waters of the ocean below, the storm kelpie churned the waves into whirlpools with her kelp wings. The roar of their laughter could not be heard over the cacophony of rushing water and resounding thunder, but the storm kelpie's face as she threw back her head and opened her mouth radiated pure joy. Together they created storms.

"Ryka anu—"

"Saving all the good songs for yourself?"

Her sister Setamíel's sharp voice cut through the song she recalled, severing the image in Nensola's mind like a slice from the spear Setamíel still carried.

"And what of it if I am?" Nensola challenged, irritation lacing her voice. "I owe my Storytelling gift to no one."

Setamíel crouched beside Nensola, balancing on her toes and leaning against her spear for support. "That's a bit of a selfish attitude, don't you think? Imagine if we all thought like that. I don't owe anyone my strength either, but I lend it to Lothilya's Protectors so our people can stay safe."

"And you're well compensated for it," noted Nensola.

"You're compensated too," Setamíel pointed out.

"Not as well as you," Nensola retorted, then immediately gulped down the guilt in her throat. Taking a deep breath, Nensola lifted her fingers from the river, gave them a little shake, scattering water droplets, and dried them on her violet dress. She turned to face her sister, noticing the edge of anger mingled with concern flashing across her eyes. "I'm sorry. I don't mean to quarrel. I know you also lend strength where you are not compensated for it, like to protect our family after Mom died. I see your point. But I was not singing something better for myself. I was singing a bittersweet ballad of an Armindí woman and a storm kelpie falling in love."

Setamíel nodded slowly, and Nensola watched the anger ebb from her gold-flecked copper eyes. "How does it end?"

"Without hope," Nensola replied, her voice bleak and flat. "Just the way you like them. One day they vanished near the Vortex maelstrom, never to be seen again."

Setamíel's eyes widened. "Vortex? Isn't that rumored to be a portal?"

"Yes, but those are only rumours," said Nensola. "Probably born from stories like this one, where people need to cling to hope, so they create an alternative explanation to assuage their grief. There is no proof of a portal in the maelstrom."

As she spoke, an image of Kit materializing in the ocean where there had been nothing but steady waves a second before splashed across her mind. He had told her of falling into a maelstrom and, instead of being crushed by the sea, resurfacing in another world. She had supplied the word for this phenomenon: *portal*. Was it so impossible that the two lovers from her story had vanished through a maelstrom portal together to another world as well? Though she would not admit it to her jaded sister, she secretly hoped the Armindí woman and storm kelpie were still alive somewhere, living out their days together and in love. Whether that hope was born out of optimism or romanticism, she wasn't sure.

"You're probably right," Setamíel agreed, twisting the butt of her spear into the soft dirt. It never took much to convince Setamíel of the absence of hope. "Still ... if I can speak honestly with you, sister—"

"You always do," interjected Nensola.

"I don't think your performance at the palace today had quite the level of inspiration Lord Eberon and Lady Leilaní were hoping for. One mage using their magic for the first time to defeat a chimera? Not quite on the same scale as a battalion of warriors having to fight a horde of bragûl."

"You know I don't get to choose the stories," said Nensola, a tense edge of defensiveness in her voice. Why did her sister always have to criticize? To find faults? "They come to me in the moment."

"I know, but I just thought maybe ... well, maybe you were scared to tell anything with more depth," said Setamíel gently, watching Nensola's eyes for a reaction. "I know you don't like performing in the palace."

"I'm always scared of losing control," Nensola whispered, eyes locked on the river. "There's no river in the palace. Nothing to siphon the voices if they become too much. Just the pressure of judging eyes waiting to see if I will slip, so their worst suspicions about me can be confirmed."

Setamíel reached out and squeezed the back of her hand. "Your people do not fear you the way you think they do. They're in awe of your gift. That's why they stare. You have come such a long way since you were a child. Mom taught you how to control your gift well. Do you really believe you'll lose control?"

"I don't want to find out. I can't." Nensola could not hide the fear cracking her voice.

Though Setamíel tightened her grip on her sister's fingers, she remained silent, contemplating the river. Nensola contemplated it too.

Kit had once asked her why the river helped but not the ocean. Why was one body of water different from the other?

Nensola loved the ocean, but rivers were natural conveyors for stories. Rivers reflected them, carried them downstream, depositing them among the rocks on their banks, burying them in the sand on their beds. The ocean was a depository of stories. Memories amassed into a fathomless pool, fragments resurfacing into living memory with the tide, but otherwise lost. Forgotten.

The stories in a river were alive, fresh, the colours and emotions sharp and vivid.

Nensola needed clarity she could control, not depths she couldn't fathom.

It was one part of her Storytelling gift she never really had to explain to Setamíel. Her practical sister understood the need for clarity and control, for guarding against certainties instead of wishing on hope.

"You know, at some point, you're going to have to accept that Mom is gone," Setamíel said, turning to hook Nensola's shifting eyes with her sharp gaze. A burning pang lanced Nensola's heart, but she held her sister's gaze. "You're never going to feel confident and in control of your gift unless you accept that she's not coming back."

"I know she's gone," Nensola whispered, unable to trust her voice not to waver at a louder pitch.

"Do you?" Setamíel probed gently. "You have always held on to hope long after it makes sense to."

"To you, any amount of hope is too much," retorted Nensola.

"That's not true. I could have done with a bit more hope in your song today. We are about to face the bragûl who raided Tariq and killed the villagers. Increasing numbers of bragûl have been sighted along our borders for months now. This is getting serious."

"Not this again!" Nensola groaned, and she leapt to her feet to pace the riverbank. "The message of prevailing against unfavourable odds was still there. It was still a story of hope."

Setamíel shook her head, loosening the braids of the tightly coiled bun wound between her brown antlers. "The hope felt hollow, Nen. Forced and displaced. And definitely unearned. The mage had no reason to feel hope. No clue or tactic or stroke of brilliance that suggested an actual solution would be thought of to make his battle against the chimera successful. You can't just materialize hope out of nothing. Success in battle against the bragûl will not be determined by my level of hope but by my skill with my spear and my battle savvy. And maybe a bit of luck. Luck is more plausible than hope."

"You're such a pessimist," Nensola scoffed.

"And you're acting dangerously naive," retorted her sister. "About the bragûl threat and your handle on your Storytelling gift. I have helped you every way I know how since Mom died, but now I must deal with this threat to our people, and I won't be here if you lose control. Maybe your feelings for Kit make you think he'll be there to save you and comfort you—"

"What are you talking about? I don't have feelings for Kit."

"—but you can't rely on him to help you either. You need to find a way to control the voices yourself, Nensola. Become your own source of strength. Or you will become the monster you fear."

"Not everyone can wear strength as armour, like you. You live behind fortress walls so nothing can touch you. Including love. But some of us *want* to feel our emotions. To experience love. To be more than just a shield. You may protect your mind and heart that way, but then everything you experience in life is a reflection."

"Isn't that how you experience life through your stories?" Setamíel shot back.

Nensola reeled, swaying on the spot as though slapped.

"I think you have somewhere to be," Nensola whispered.

Setamíel raised her chin at the dismissal. Without a word, she turned on her heel and stalked away from the stream and her sister. But before she vanished among the trees, she paused and spoke over her shoulder.

"We can figure this out when I get back, Nensola. Together."

Setamíel's antlers were barely visible still between the aspens when Nensola shouted, "Good luck!"

Weaving the *hibinco* plant fibres with deft fingers, Nensola twisted and braided them into a strong, thin rope, a chore she had been practising since childhood. Short and stubby, her father's rough fingers knotted her completed strands into place, repairing a tear in one of his fishing nets. Their busy hands created a soft rhythm, a murmured duet of mutual comfort as they worked side by side. The steady rhythm helped distract her from her tumultuous thoughts, calming the waves of fury threatening to rise beneath her calm exterior, though it couldn't entirely smooth out the scowl tugging at her lips.

"How did the performance at the palace go?" her father asked, eyes locked on his work.

A muscle twitched in Nensola's jaw, but her fingers continued weaving. "Fine enough."

"Everyone seemed inspired?" her father asked, his tone casual. Too casual. "They're all ready to go fight the bragûl now?"

Nensola's fingers froze. She pierced his bowed antlered head with a glare, and his fingers slipped over the next knot.

"Did Setamíel stop by here before she went off to battle?" Nensola demanded.

"No. I haven't seen your sister since you two left for the palace this morning. I know I'm not the most observant father in the world, but give me some credit. Even I can see the storm cloud hovering over you."

Nensola let her muscles relax into the scowl tugging at them.

With a heavy sigh, her father draped the net gently over the driftwood table and gave his daughter his full attention.

"What happened? Did you and your sister quarrel?"

"Possibly." The jut of Nensola's jaw signalled both a defence and a challenge.

"Look, I'm not going to pry the details out of you if you don't want to tell me, but you know your sister cares for you, right? She's not always the most eloquent—gets that from me, I guess—but her heart's in a good place."

"Then why does she criticize me so much?" huffed Nensola. "She isn't different, like me. She's not a Storyteller; she doesn't still resemble a peryton too much. She doesn't know what it's like. She just thinks I'm weak."

Her father grasped her shoulder, fingers grazing the bone where her wings jutted out.

"She doesn't think you're weak, Nensola. No one does. She's just trying to protect you. She's scared for you. She knows your wings are coveted. A commodity people will kill for. The reason they killed your mother. If your sister is overprotective of you, it's my fault," her father continued, and Nensola could hear the catch in his throat, see the tears gloss his eyes. "I couldn't protect your mother when the pirates came for her wings. Setamíel worries I won't be able to protect you either. She became a warrior to make up for *my* weakness, not yours."

"Father ..." Nensola began, wrapping her arms around his shaking chest. "No one blames you for Mother's death."

"I do. Setamíel does. And while that's nice of you to say, I'm sure you do too. It's all right," he assured her, his chest rattling against hers as he took a deep, shuddering breath. "My failings should be my burden to bear alone. Already you girls do too much bearing it with me. Setamíel thinks she needs to be both mother and father instead of just your sister. It clouds her judgment sometimes. But she does love you."

"I know," Nensola murmured. She pulled away awkwardly, the ghost of her mother sliding between them again. An emotional buffer to ensure they didn't let their guard down.

"Come, that's enough with the nets for today," said her father, carefully rolling up the net so it wouldn't tangle and packing the extra *hibinco* fibres into a basket. "Let's start preparing dinner!"

If mending nets was a murmured duet, cooking dinner was a sonorous drum duel, a booming battle of innate talent and bravado. The rhythmic slapping of her father's hands as he pounded seasoning into the cleaned and gutted fish faded to a background beat beneath Nensola's sharp, fast chopping of zucchini, peppers, and *apana* leaves. The sizzling of frying fish competed with the staccato spitting of roasting vegetables. Bubbling, boiling *qir'a* grains clashed with the hissing of steaming frond bowls. Only when the ingredients had been prepared and they had spooned the fish and vegetables onto a bed of *qir'a* grains served in a frond bowl did they find harmonious equilibrium.

A fond smile softened Nensola's face when her father sat across from her and raised his spun-coral fork at his daughter in a gesture of thanks for her contributions to their practised dance. He never took anything for granted.

Her first forkful of dinner was halfway to her mouth when a knock disturbed their peaceful meal, and her father pulled open the door to reveal Kit.

Instead of putting the fork down, Nensola shoved the steaming grains hastily into her mouth and burned her tongue. Eyes widening, she forced her numb tongue to push the grains back and swallow, and they scalded her throat on the way down as well.

"Kit," she choked out hoarsely, pretending not to notice the laugh he tried to quell. Clearing her throat, she tried again. "Kit, how are you?"

"*Vair nor*," he said to her father with a nod of his head. Then he turned to Nensola. "I just returned from our trip to Stillwater Reef, on the border of Voita. I know I should have come tomorrow, but I couldn't wait to see you. I have so much to share with you."

Heart fluttering at the raw sincerity in Kit's stormy grey eyes, Nensola glanced at her father before replying. A subtle twitch of his lips and a crinkle at the corners of his eyes compromised his steadily neutral gaze and stoic pose.

"I'm glad you came, Kit. Would you like to join us for dinner?"

"Yes, if it's all right with your father. I haven't eaten since dawn. I'm famished."

"Sit," said her father, gesturing to a woven mat beside him. His broken, monosyllabic English had improved vastly over the last year but still paled in comparison with Nensola's fluidity. Kit had been delighted to discover Nensola's affinity with words and language. He had been teaching her both English and Spanish almost every day in exchange for lessons in Tavé, the language of the Lantíé. His clumsy Tavé made it easy to advocate for the necessity of repetition, even if they spent some lectures more preoccupied with stealing glances at each other.

"*Ûnn es, ada,*" Kit replied formally to her father, folding his long limbs awkwardly onto the square mat while her father scooped dinner into a frond bowl and set it before his guest.

"Did you catch many fish?" Nensola's father asked between bites. His casual tone barely hid the anticipation shining in his eyes. Nensola knew he planned his own fishing expedition up the coast in the next fortnight, and she had noticed the concern lacing his voice whenever the trip was brought up.

"Yes, Master Metka was very pleased with the catch. The fish supply is as plentiful as ever," Kit assured her father. His shoulders relaxed, his chest visibly deflating in relief. "But we couldn't linger near Voita long. It's a sinister and foreboding forest at the best of times, but this time ... even from the water, we could see the black tendrils snaking from the roots. And from between the trees, streaks of black smudging the shadows, trailing wisps blurring the dark hollows ... and flashes of blood red or eerie yellow blinking at us ..."

"Bragûl," whispered Nensola and her father in unison.

Kit looked between them, his lips a thin line. "That's what Master Metka thought too."

"They have been raiding Lothilya's borders," Nensola informed Kit. "Setamíel left with a band of warriors to fight them today."

Nensola's voice did not waver, exactly, but it must have snagged on her sister's name a little. Kit shot her a sharp look, searching her eyes to confirm the emotion catching her voice. Worry? Or anger? Nensola didn't even know. She offered him a small smile to show she was fine, but his tight lips told her he could see the melancholy strain of her muscles.

Silence settled over them as they ate. Kit kept stealing glances at Nensola, but she avoided meeting his eyes. His concern for her would pass if she didn't validate it.

But when Nensola had eaten her last bite, Kit asked, "Would you like to join me for a walk, Nensola? That is, if it's all right with your father."

Her father's indulgent smile bristled her wing feathers a little as he nodded his consent.

Unfolding her wings, Nensola rose from her mat and said, "A walk sounds lovely."

Torchlight suffused the darkness around their huts, blinding her with a bright orange glow when she first stepped out into the night. Raising her wing to shield her eyes, she followed Kit's boots until they reached the sand beyond the homes. He paused, taking off his boots so he could walk barefoot in the sand as well. Nensola kept her eyes down, following his lead until she felt the cool, smooth grains of wet sand between her toes. She lowered her wing and breathed deeply, drinking in the softened glow of natural lights. No torches were needed here.

Luminous wonders illuminated the turquoise reef. Tiny organisms too minuscule to see in daylight lit up the foamy surf at night like a sea of electric-blue and white stars. Sprays of violet and fuchsia ignited tangled beds of coral, and sparkling sapphire fish flashed past the teal suckers of an octopus's groping tentacles. Translucent jellyfish glowed white as they engaged in a languid, mesmerizing moonlit dance. The pearly sheen of a full moon reflected on the deep, rippling indigo ocean. A plethora of stars blanketed the cloudless sky, sparkling among a swath of a misty galaxy.

Nensola's eyes lingered on the stars. A thread pulled deep within her chest, tugging on her soul. Beckoning her to open herself up to the cosmos, to succumb to the voices calling to her there. Stomach fluttering, she forced her eyes to fixate on the pulsating jellyfish instead. Whether the stars beckoned her to recall stories of the cosmos through her Storytelling gift, or whether a deep-rooted longing to commune with Celestial magic and find souls from parallel worlds to consume, like her peryton ancestors had, awakened, she did not know. And she did not want to find out.

"Are you worried about your sister?" Kit asked without preamble.

A hollow chuckle escaped Nensola's lips. "My sister knows how to protect and defend. It's what she does best. I'm not worried about her in battle, but … we fought today, after I performed for the departing band of warriors at the palace. Setamíel didn't think my song was good enough."

"Ah," said Kit. He waited, knowing her well enough to know there was more.

"She can be such a hypocrite, but … I hate that we quarreled right before she left for battle. It just … leaves a sour taste in my mouth. I would hate her thoughts to be tainted by anger toward me while she's fighting."

Nensola kicked at the sand, splashing her toes in the chilly surf.

"Setamíel will be fine," Kit assured her gently. "She's too smart to let her stubborn anger cloud her judgment. And she loves you."

He traced a heart in the sand with his toe. Nensola laughed and splashed him playfully.

"I know, you're right. I already feel better out here, away from those glaring torches."

"You would not enjoy living in a city like London," Kit observed, laughing. "I've only been there once, on business with my father, but at night the lights are so numerous, and the city fumes so thick, that it can blot out the stars."

"You can't see them at all?" Nensola asked in horror. Her lungs ached at the idea of a world without stars.

"You can still see them, but not as bright, and not as many. It disturbed me too. I'm so used to navigating a course with stars. Without all of them, I felt lost. I was so relieved to find the stars were familiar here, even if they have different names. It's comforting when things are familiar, but different."

Catching the weight of his last words, Nensola turned to see his expression—and found him looking at her, the whirlpool of his eyes drawing her in, directing her attention to the storm clouds of his irises, heavy with the words left unspoken. The words that teetered more on the brink of pouring out the longer this moment stretched.

"This is where we first met," Nensola whispered. "Do you ... do you miss home?"

Kit traced her cheekbone and trailed his fingers down her jawline. She shivered at the touch, every nerve in her body alert and tingling. He cupped her cheek, and she leaned into the warmth of his palm.

"Not when I'm with you," he breathed back.

Kit tilted her chin up so her antlers wouldn't tangle in his hair, and his lips found hers. Slanting over them slowly at first, learning their shape. The way their lips fit together. His strong arms wrapped around her, brushing the feathers of her wings, and she buried her fingers in his windswept hair. The kiss deepened, and warmth blossomed low in Nensola's belly.

Nensola spread her wings wide, then folded them around Kit, enveloping him like a cocoon.

Preserving this moment for just the two of them.

It was just a kiss.

But somehow Nensola knew when they emerged from this moment, everything would change.

The soft, warm glow of dawn kissed Nensola awake the next morning, and she opened her eyes with a smile on her lips. After rolling over in her hammock, she traced the echo of Kit's kiss with her fingertips, trailing them over the warmth still lingering on her lips. A deep contentment filled Nensola's heart, like the comforting weight of Kit's arms wrapped around her.

She carried the warm glow of their kiss with her like a whispered secret all morning. While she unbraided her hair, letting the teal strands hang in loose curls down her back. While she prepared their morning meal with her father, laughing when the tip of her wing accidentally knocked over the bowl of fruit she had just sliced. Even when someone knocked on the door, and it wasn't Kit.

It was a Lantian soldier, carrying no weapon but still clad in bloodstained armour.

The bubble of contentment buoying Nensola's spirits burst. A painful pit hollowed her stomach. The warm glow turned to ice, freezing the breath in her chest.

Her numb brain watched the messenger form Setamíel's name on her lips.

Killed in the battle with the bragûl.

Dead.

Voices flooded Nensola's head. Black spots blurred her vision. Pain slashed at her lungs, and she struggled to breathe. Dark shadows spread across her soul.

And she was powerless to stop them.

Four

A low mist clung to the banks of the stream behind Nensola's home, dewdrops bejewelling the blades of grass and dampening the seat of Kit's breeches, but he didn't complain. This morning, all complaints floated downstream, washed away by Nensola's overpowering grief.

When he had knocked on her door to greet her with a teal-threaded violet spiral shell he had found on the beach that reminded him of her, he had been hoping his romantic gesture would earn him another kiss. Instead, he had been greeted with the shell of Nensola. Vacant red eyes hollowed by sorrow, emptied of romance. Tears staining her cheeks in place of a dimpled smile. Memories of warm embraces replaced by the icy clutches of death.

His chest had tightened, burning with a blunt ache at the sight of her pain.

Before he could ask what was wrong, her eyes had widened, pupils dilating in manic fear, and she had grabbed his arm and yanked him through the house and out the back door. Heart thudding erratically in his ears, hairs rising on his arms, Kit had shouted, "Nensola, what's wrong? Talk to me!"

But she had just run to the stream, cast herself on the bank, and shoved her arm in the water. Lying on her stomach, wings sweeping the dew as she folded them awkwardly behind her, Nensola had closed her eyes in relief—then burst into tears.

Taking her free hand, Kit had squeezed it, not knowing what else to do but needing to comfort her somehow, lend her the strength to fight the onslaught of voices he knew must be assaulting her mind if she was attempting to siphon them off in the stream. Her tears had mingled with the dewdrops, muddying the bank, which had then stained her temple with dirt.

When her eyes had emptied of tears and her sobs had subsided to ragged breaths, Nensola had sat up, still clinging to his hand like a lost child, and spoken the three most raw, tortured words Kit had ever heard her choke out.

"Setamíel is dead."

A dull blow had hollowed his stomach. A serrated swallow had raked his throat.

He hadn't known what to say.

He still didn't.

He just squeezed her hand and stroked the dip between her pointer finger and thumb with his own thumb in slow, soothing circles. Listening to the stream's loud chatter breaking the silence for him. Knowing silence would not be enough.

"Do you know how it happened?"

"Why is that always the first thing people ask?" Nensola asked, shaking her head. "As if the *how* matters when a piece of your soul is lost. As if a peaceful instead of a violent death would lessen the agony tormenting the griever's every waking moment. The pain is still raw and visceral and unyielding, regardless of the *how*."

The wrong thing to say. Clearly.

"You're right. Of course, you're right. I'm sorry, Nensola. Sorry for asking that, and so, so sorry for your sister's death," said Kit, but even to his ears, it sounded like a hollow platitude.

He wanted to offer her more, be more for her than just another vessel of empty words. But he didn't know how. When his parents had died, all he had received from anyone was empty platitudes. Barren promises of religious salvation. Futile assurances that everything would be all right. No one had shown him an alternative way to console someone grieving. Maybe there *was* no alternative.

Death was finite. Absolute.

What words had the power to undo the irreversible?

"We don't know how it happened yet," Nensola said after a moment, like an offer to accept his apology. She still kept her fingers intertwined with his. "Father left for the palace just before you arrived, to find out more information. He was ... not all right. I'm not all right. I don't even know how to describe how I feel. Setamíel was our rock. Daughter, sister, mother, but also provider, partner, and protector. Without her our family ... without her *I* will be ..."

"Overwhelmed? Lost? Exposed? Like you're adrift at sea, looking for an anchor?" Kit supplied.

Nensola searched his face, misted seafoam eyes locking on his intently like she was truly seeing him for the first time. She stroked the curve of his hand with her thumb.

"Yes," she breathed. "That's how you felt when your parents died?"

Kit nodded, rolling a blade of grass between his fingers with his free hand.

"With my mom even more than my dad. Maybe I asked you how it happened because the how sort of did matter with me. My dad was brutally murdered right in front of me. I was traumatized. Part of me broken and scarred forever. But the grief felt different than it did with my mom's death. I understood the racial injustice with my dad's death. The corruption and hate that fueled his murderers blazed within me, a raging inferno that burned the edges of my grief and furled my pain. My mom's death didn't elicit the same rage. Just more emptiness. A vast hole for the grief to pour into and fill."

"What did you do to drain the hole and close it?" Nensola asked, and Kit flinched at the desperation strangling her voice. He hated disappointing her.

"Nothing," he whispered. "There's no magic stopper for your grief. All you can do is patch the hole. Slow the rush of sorrow. Make it less overwhelming. And hope you find your anchor one day."

Kit reached into the deep pocket of the light coat he wore fishing and pulled out the longitude device he had stolen from his father. He still marveled that it had not only survived the fall through the portal but actually worked in this world. Measuring longitude was a navigational challenge on the Tolotanteau as well, and the device's accuracy on his sailing ventures up and down the coast of Carmelle had earned Kit the trust of Lothilyan sailors, enough to ensure he was never short of work. He fiddled with the dial, thinking of Captain Firth. Did Kit have another death to mourn without even knowing about it?

Nensola barked a bitter, hollow laugh. "I have always need-ed an anchor. To keep me from getting lost in the sea of voices clamouring inside my head. To stop them from pulling me under. Drowning me. Grief makes it so much worse. Anger became my shield after my mom's death as well. The weapon I armed myself with against both external and internal demons. But I can't find a weapon this time. I can't ... I can't control the stories by myself. I feel a madness creeping in. A shadow stalking my soul."

"Maybe some closure could help," Kit ventured, becoming practical in the absence of a solution against soul shadows. He flicked the longitude device's dial a little too hard, and he cursed and fumbled it when it sprang back at him. "H-how do the Lantíé mourn? Do you bury your dead, or ...?"

Heat flooded his cheeks, but he forced himself to keep looking at Nensola instead of letting his embarrassment breed cowardice. He feared his question might be inappropriate or impertinent, but because he knew Lantíes were immortal unless killed by disease or fatal wounds, he had never discussed how Lantíes mourned their dead. What had they done with Nensola's mother's body? Maybe a formal ritual of acknowledging Setamíel's life and death could bring Nensola a measure of comfort.

Taking a deep, shaky breath, Nensola then answered through quivering lips. "I-if we can recover Setamíel's body, we will float her out to Aspengrove Island, the island home of our Lothilyan ancestors, at sunset. After floating her around the island while singing a dirge of her life under the blooming stars, her soul will be released to dance among the cosmos. And finally, at sunrise, her body will be tied and returned to the ocean to protect the balance of life in Arwé."

"That sounds like a fitting way to honour her life," said Kit gently. He tapped his finger against the longitude device, already planning a way he could help her through the ceremony. Paddle her out to the island, hold her hand during the dirge, especially if she sang it. Wrap her in his arms as they laid Setamíel to rest in the ocean. Be her rock in the storm ...

"Will you stop with that?" Nensola burst exasperatedly, gesturing a wing toward the longitude device. "You're going to break it!"

Kit's cheeks burned hotter than the sun.

"Are you always that careless with things loved ones give you?" Nensola challenged.

"Of course not! I am just nervous ... I'm sorry," Kit replied. "Although, technically, my father didn't *give* it to me. It's not a treasured heirloom or something. I just took it. To protect him, though. Because he stole it. And his plan to sell it was going to get him killed. And I couldn't let him die to protect me and his crew.

He was being stubborn. Taking risks. I guess I was too. But no one shows a pirate mercy."

Clamping his mouth shut, Kit bit his rambling tongue and inwardly cursed his stupidity, refraining from hiding his face in his hands. For a year, he had avoided saying the word *pirate*, wanting to start life in Carmelle unburdened by the preconceived prejudices of labels. Maybe she hadn't noticed.

But Nensola's eyes widened, then narrowed beneath her furrowed brows, scanning Kit's face like she didn't recognize him. Nostrils flaring in disgust, the corners of her mouth turning down, she leaned back and dropped his hand. Recoiling from him.

"You're a ... pirate?"

The word dripped vitriol, tainted with a venom reserved for despicable, deplorable deeds.

Numbness stole through Kit's veins, paralyzing his body. A vise tightened around his chest, squeezing his lungs. He couldn't breathe. Couldn't speak. Could only feel the tingling in his hand, the absence of her touch.

Nensola leapt to her feet, spread her wings to their full breadth and inclined her head slightly, pointing her antlers at him. A stance to combat fear. To push it down beneath a show of bravery. To prepare herself to act, not react. To attack.

Kit gaped at the swell of her seafoam eyes, the hate building behind the fear, ready to furl over and drown him.

"Nensola," he choked out. A desperate plea.

"GET AWAY!" she screamed, taking a step toward him. "Get away, *pirate*!"

She flung the word at him like a contaminated spear, spat it like poison she needed to cleanse from her body.

He shuffled back a bit with his hands and feet like a crab before he stood. But he didn't leave yet. The memory of their kiss still hung in the air, fluttering between them like a winged secret. He could still taste her lips, feel the warm weight of her pressed against him. Hear the soft *shush* of her wings as they folded around him, silencing the outside world so only the two of them existed in that moment.

He took a step toward her.

For a moment, she stood perfectly still, maybe feeling the echo of his lips grazing hers.

Then she beat her wings, *hard*, pumping air at him and buffeting him back.

"Stay away from me!" Nensola shouted through sobs, her chest heaving. "I don't want to see you here ever again! You are *not* welcome in Lothilya, or anywhere in Arwé. Go back through the portal!"

Pain bubbled in Kit's chest, boiling against the unyielding vise grip that squeezed his lungs. Head swimming, vision blurring, he drank in gulps of air before the pressure closed his throat again, and he ran. He ran away from her house, away from her village. Away from the happiness he had almost achieved. He ran Away.

Unwelcome among the Lantíe. Unwelcome among the British or Spanish. Unmoored. Unanchored. Forever adrift at sea. That was his destiny.

Setamíel had been right, Nensola thought, cradling her head in her hands. Hope had forsaken them. It was madness to hope people would change—to hope they could be different, if only given the chance. Opening your heart to the ideal of possibility was not heroic or brave. It was naive and stupid.

She could see Setamíel now, shaking her head with affectionate indulgence. *I warned you not to trust him*, she would say.

Setamíel had been very wary of Kit when Nensola had first introduced him. She had barraged Nensola with questions in Tavé. "Where did he come from? If he's not from Carmelle, where is he from? Humans don't just drop from the sky or sprout from the ground like invasive plants. If he's from another world, he must have a reason for being here. What does he want?"

Though Nensola had asked herself the same questions, her answers had never been to her practical, logical sister's liking. "He has no interest in avenging some distant ancestor one of our peryton ancestors may or may not have killed when harvesting souls from other worlds, Setamíel. He doesn't even know who we are. People do drop from the sky or sprout from the ground when they come through portals. And they don't need a reason to be here. I have recalled enough portal stories to know they often come through accidentally. If he wants to show us kindness, the least we can do is reciprocate. I'd rather not confirm people's worst suspicions about me."

Kit had sensed her distrust right away, so he had tried hard to win her favour—always excessively polite, rushing to help her or bring her favourite food when he came to visit, or even cracking jokes to make her smile. Eventually, Setamíel had come to view Kit as a brother.

But Setamíel's instincts had been right. Kit should not have been trusted.

Pirate.

Nensola rolled the bitter word along her tongue, saliva building against its vile taste.

She had never shared the specifics of her mother's death with Kit. She had told him her mother had been murdered in her own home, right in front of her, and that had been enough. Kit hadn't asked the specifics, because he didn't need to know. He had told her his father had been murdered in front of him in the same way, and that shared moment of pain and trauma had forged a bond needing no further words.

Or so she had thought at the time. Maybe if she had said the word *pirate*, things would have been different between them.

Pirates wanted her wings for the magic in her feathers. They had murdered a Lantíé to steal her wings, depriving a husband of a wife and children of a mother, all for the sake of filling their pockets. Their arrogance entitled them to strip people of their identity, stealing their essence, their soul. Nensola didn't care if they were starving and needed the money for survival. She didn't care if they had families of their own to provide for. She didn't care if pirates on Earth were different from the pirates who had murdered her mother. She didn't care if Kit's father had stolen to protect his son, didn't care if his intentions were honourable and his sword clean.

She loathed pirates.

Betrayal stabbed her heart, slicing through it with a serrated edge. Her best friend, the person she had cared for most besides her family, had transformed into her enemy in the space of a second. From one breath to the next, pleasure at the feel of his fingers entwined with hers had morphed into acute pain. Heavy weight pushed her shoulders down, crushing her chest, pulling her to her knees with the gravity of grief.

Hours later, when her father came home from the palace, he found her curled in the corner, hair tangled in her antlers, wings cocooning a body that would not unbend.

Nensola heard the shuffle of his feet. Rocked a little as his shoulder bumped her wing when he sat beside her. Closed her eyes at his soft touch as his fingers worked to untangle her hair from her antlers, stroking it away from her face.

"They haven't found her body yet," he said into the silence.

Nensola blinked, another dull blow thumping her heart, but said nothing.

"I talked to Lord Eberon," her father continued, unperturbed by her silence. "A fellow Lantian warrior took her pulse during battle when they found her body. She *is* dead. But the bodies of the fallen seem to have been dragged off somewhere by the bragûl. Lord Eberon didn't know why. But they do know there is someone behind these bragûl attacks. A woman was at the battle. Leading the bragûl. Wielding magic. They say she's the one who killed Setamíel. The woman escaped alive."

Slowly Nensola sat up, searching her father's sorrowful eyes for information he might be withholding. But only grief reflected back at her, and something more primal. A simmering desire for revenge.

A spark ignited deep within Nensola, flickering with a mirrored heat of vengeance.

After a moment, her father asked, "Will Kit be coming for dinner tonight?"

"No," Nensola replied flatly, her voice dull and emotionless. "Kit won't be coming for dinner ever again. He's a pirate."

Five

K it dipped his paddle into the rolling water and pulled it toward him slowly, careful not to scatter droplets across the surface like skipping stones and create more ripples. Already the ocean's stubborn determination to remain opaque past the reef ground Kit's teeth. How was he supposed to find the portal if he couldn't see more than a few inches beyond the damn surface?

Nensola's message still clanged in his ears like cymbals. Hope she would change her mind had evaporated with her rejection of his desperate pleas at the market this morning. Again.

If she couldn't forgive him, if she found his mere presence in her vicinity so abhorrent, then he wouldn't force her to suffer. He would leave. He could stay in Arwé, move somewhere else in Carmelle, but he would always want to return to Lothilya. He would always want to be with her. And if that couldn't be … he may as well go back to Earth and find his father.

If he could ever find the portal.

Cursing under his breath, Kit secured the paddle to the small, shallow wooden boat, the type the Lantíés favoured for short single-paddle excursions around the reef, then swivelled his legs over the side and slipped into the sea. A chilly current billowed up from the depths and washed over his skin, constricting his chest. Salt water assaulted his eyes, but Kit ignored the stinging burn and kept them open. Looking over his shoulder occasionally to ensure his boat didn't drift too far, he peered through the dark, murky water for a sign of the portal.

He had been so sure the maelstrom had brought him to this area of Crescent Bay. He could see the rock Nensola had emerged from behind to greet him that first day, though the bay *was* big, the rock visible from many vantage points. And he had been tossed and tumbled by the waves so much it was hard to say where his head had first broken the surface.

Searching the patches of ocean lit by sunbeams, Kit kicked his legs wide like a frog, twisting his body whenever he thought glistening bubbles might be shimmers of a portal. Soon his lungs ached, so he kicked to the surface and grabbed onto the boat to catch his breath. Taking a deep gulp of air, he started to duck back under—only to be pummeled by a small wave. Water spilled into his open mouth, and the wave pushed him under, battering his shoulders and wrenching his hand from its grip on his boat.

Arms and legs flailing, Kit struggled to regain control, to find the surface again in the tumultuous turmoil. A thick cloud of wave bubbles obscured the sunlight, but they soon thinned, and Kit's head broke the surface. Overcome with coughs to rid his heaving lungs of water, Kit reached for the boat so he didn't have to tread water—and felt only air. Spinning in a circle, he scanned the choppy surface until he spotted it thirty feet away.

Kit unleashed a frustrated scream and slapped the water. *This is ridiculous! What am I even doing out here? Of course I can't find a portal this way!*

This wasn't the first time he had tried. His search ended a little sooner each time, as he convinced himself more easily that the effort was fruitless. Swimming with his head out of the water to make sure he didn't lose sight of the boat, Kit closed the distance, then heaved himself back into it. Sopping wet and dripping rivulets into a pool at his feet, he paddled hard toward shore, his strokes strong and confident.

Unlike his mind. A muddled haze of anger and despair fogged his brain, clouding his judgment. He didn't know what to do. Piracy lacked honour, and he could understand Nensola's disdain for the trade, but her rage and loathing confused him. Whatever her experience with pirates, it had caused her to paint them all with the same blackened brush. But not all pirates were corrupt. *He* wasn't corrupt.

Was he?

A few feet from his boat, a fennik frolicked in the waves with its pup, twisting and dipping below the surface with its sleek, lithe body like an otter. Their sopping indigo fur blended in with the deep amethysts and magentas of the sunset, the playful swish of their three-pronged bushy tails swirling the last vermilion sparkles of sunlight. Every splash of Kit's paddle warranted a twitch of their long, pointy, foxlike ears, but they otherwise ignored his presence.

This was why he hadn't wanted to tell Nensola his father was a pirate, or that he had been complicit in his father's schemes. Telling her he was a sailor delivering the longitude device for a prize had still been true. He just hadn't seen any reason to include the part about stealing the device. He hadn't known how Nensola would react, and he hadn't wanted to have to question if he was corrupt anymore. He wanted to live on the margins of morally grey instead of being mired in it. Start fresh, with a clean slate.

He had always thought he needed to be Spanish or English, but not both. He could choose piracy, like his father, or be an honourable man, but not both. His heart could be full of hate or full of hope, but not both.

But dichotomy didn't have to mean division. Contradictions could coexist in a person. Thrive, even. When he had come to Carmelle, he could just be himself, in all his dichotomous complexities, and people had accepted him. Nensola had accepted him. With her, he felt whole. At home.

He wasn't ready to let that feeling go.

The last deep burnished-copper rays of the setting sun glinted off the obsidian roofs of Lothilya, prompting Kit to shield his eyes with one arm while paddling closer to the city with the other. Aspen docks lined the peninsula from Lothilya's western borders, halfway out onto the peninsula, to its eastern border, in the forest dividing the main city from the outlying villages, like Nensola's. But Kit headed away from Nensola's village, toward the westernmost dock, the last one before the expanse of barren black rock separating the city from the palace. Eyes fixated on a cylindrical birch-bark house with a domed obsidian roof halfway up the craggy hill, Kit ignored the last ray of vanishing sun and the deepening blue of encroaching twilight. He ignored the possibility that it was rapidly approaching too late to do this today.

When he reached the dock, Kit barely spared enough time to tie his boat and leave his name with the dockmaster before sprinting barefoot across the rest of the dock and up the steep, curved path winding its way through the cliffside streets. Sharp pebbles stabbed his tender soles, but he only stopped to brush the worst of them off every few minutes. A few Lantíés snickered at his quick, jilted steps and wobbly knees when they watched him stumble by their homes, then rushed to help, but Kit waved them off. He focused on the way the houses mimicked both the ocean and the forest dwellings of their ancestors instead of his pain.

Birch, aspen, and driftwood logs were amalgamated with walls of foamy pumice and clay. Obsidian roofs crowned city homes, and woven palm-frond roofs topped village homes and awnings. Alone and exposed at the tip of the peninsula, the palace's turrets of melded, glossy shells shone in a palette of whites, ivories, deep purples, and pale pinks. Accents of tiled sea gems bordered windows and doors. Kit had never set foot inside the palace, but he hoped to one day. Even from the outside, the staggered rows of obsidian domed towers nestled among the jagged black rocks of the cliff bespoke an architectural marvel.

His panting gasps as he crested a hill and spotted the birch house he had seen from the shore looming only a few feet above him persuaded him to pause, catch his breath, and slow his heart rate. At least the captain of Lothilya's Protectors didn't live in one of the houses on the southern cliffs of the peninsula. Built into recesses in the treacherous cliff face just above the reach of storm waves, they were accessible only by flying or climbing.

Lantern light glowed through the transparent netted window, indicating the captain was home, and presumably awake. A small miracle, given the constant bragûl attacks. Wiping the blood from his feet and the sweat from his brow, he then wrung the excess water from his shirt and squared his shoulders.

He needed Nensola to see him for who he truly was, to accept and embrace every facet of him, good and bad. She knew the bad now. She knew the duplicitous, selfish tendencies of his pirating ways. And even if Kit didn't fully understand her intense loathing for pirates, he needed to try to show her the good. Show her he was selfish sometimes, just like everyone else, but that he could also be altruistic. He would never intentionally hurt her.

Lothilya needed defenders. He could take Setamíel's place, defend the Lantíes he had grown to love, and Nensola's family. Fight for the right to call this his home.

She didn't need his protection. But he could show her his loyalty.

For a moment, when he reached the captain's door, he hesitated with his fist raised to knock. Was pirate worse than warrior? Kit's stomach gurgled and squirmed at the thought of replacing one fallacy with another. Maybe the difference was just in semantics, but he was willing to find out.

He knocked.

The whirring hum of night insects filled the silence while Kit held his breath, waiting. Tired feet shuffled across the stone floor behind the door. Then the door swung open, spilling light into the darkness. A tall, broad-shouldered Lantié peered out at him, harrowed eyes narrowed. Short, thick antlers helmeted his head.

"Captain Ní-brik?" asked Kit. He had overheard the captain's name many times in the last year but had never met him.

Grunting, the captain nodded his head in acknowledgement.

"I want to join the Protectors," Kit said without preamble in Tavé. "I want to help protect Lothilya."

Folding his arms across his barrel chest, the captain surveyed Kit from head to toe, taking in the soggy fisherman's clothes, bare feet caked with dirt and blood, and lack of pointed ears, antlers, or anything to mark him as Lantian instead of human.

"You don't look like a soldier," the captain remarked doubtfully, answering in Tavé. "And why would you want to protect Lantié and the people of Lothilya when you're human?"

"You're right. I'm not a soldier. I'm a fisherman. But I can wield a sword. And Lothilya is my home. I have lived here for a year, and I care about her fate, and the fate of her people. I would be honoured to protect Lothilya."

The captain held Kit's eyes for a long moment, searching them for the qualities and merits his warriors must possess. Kit's throat bobbed, attempting to swallow saliva that had dried up, and he tried not to blink.

Finally the captain smiled and said, "I see you have heart, and courage. Volunteers are rare these days. If you would like to trade a fishing pole for a sword, I would be glad of an extra defender."

Though his muscles did not seem to remember how to smile, Kit's shoulders slumped and his chest loosened, the tension gripping his torso releasing its hold.

He was not adrift yet. He had been thrown a rope, and he would cling to it until his anchor found its hold.

Kit adjusted his *hibinco*-fibre mail shirt and rolled his shoulders beneath light metal pauldrons. He shifted his spear in one hand and gripped the pommel of the sword girded at his hip with the other, trying to appease his fidgeting fingers while still maintaining an outward appearance of calm. Judging by the sideways glances of the Lantian Protectors marching beside him, he was failing. Discomfort itched in every part of his body. His skin did not feel like his own, and he wanted to shed it like a snake.

Despite the weeks of rigorous training Captain Ní-brik had accelerated him through, Kit's confidence waned with every step he took. Luckily, the lightweight Lantian sword proved similar enough to the rapier he had used on Earth, but he had never used anything like the spear, and it still fit awkwardly in his hand. And pirate raids and skirmishes had ill prepared him for a coordinated battle with a group of skilled warriors.

Concentrating on Nensola, he pictured the pain cresting her seafoam eyes, the hurt in her recoiled body. He felt the warmth of her embrace, the tender brush of a wing against his cheek. He almost closed his eyes to savour the memory but thought better of it. He needed to stay alert. The bragûl could be hiding among the trees, blending in with the shadows. Ready to strike the unsuspecting. And though he had heard descriptions of them from Nensola, he had never seen one before. What if he didn't recognize them until it was too late?

A branch cracked beneath his boot, and he jumped.

"Relax, Kit," groaned Ekina from beside him. "The bragûl don't know we're coming. *We* have the element of surprise."

"Right," Kit mumbled, but he found no consolation in her words. The Protectors had been foiled by this logic before. Ekina had paid for her trust in tactics when their plan had gone awry the day Setamíel had been killed. Kit doubted whether the Lothilyans knew how to handle these attacks. Captain Ní-brik had admitted they had not been able to discern a pattern. Every time their spies located the bragûl and they thought their attack was pre-emptive, the bragûl were ready for them. Maybe the sour memory of her friend's death was what puckered Ekina's lips now.

But then they curled into a wry smile, and Ekina added, "Besides, the real warning sign of a bragûl attack is silence. They're too stealthy to do anything as clumsy as cracking a branch."

Kit's stomach plummeted, and he scanned the silver-white birches and aspens of the forest with wide eyes.

Ekina's snort of laughter ricocheted off the trees, bouncing around the clearing they had just walked into.

The hairs on Kit's arms rose. The absence of trees unnerved him. He hunched his shoulders against the oppressive vulnerability.

At the front of the group, Captain Ní-brik raised a gauntleted fist, and the company halted. He scanned the clearing, moving only his head. Kit peered into the gaps between trees, looking for irregular movement among the dancing shadows of sun-dappled leaves.

A deeper shadow shifted behind a thick trunk. Blacker than the rest. Separating from the natural, sun-induced shadows. And at its darkest point, a flash of red.

Like a blinking eye.

Kit's head and heart pounded in unison, racing to meet at his throat, burning the word of warning as it passed between his lips in a strangled shout. "Bragûl!"

Pouring from between the trees like oil spilled from a barrel, the bragûl surged toward the Protectors, shadowy black wisps trailing from their smudged bodies as they ran, making it impossible to discern their corporeal form. Blood-red and eerie-yellow eyes blazed above their open black maws, lined with layered rows of sharp teeth. They wore no armour, relying on their speed and dexterity to protect them. But they bore weapons. Clawed fingers brandished twisted, jagged swords and daggers. They broke upon the Lantíés like an ebony wave—but the Lantíés were ready for them.

Spears hurled into the onslaught of mingling shadows and sleek, bony bodies, some slicing through several bragûl at a time. Kit hefted his spear and aimed it at the bragûl he had spotted in the trees, but another bragûl reached him first and severed his spear in two. Kit drew his sword and raised it just enough to block the bragûl's stab at his heart. Undeterred, the bragûl dropped its dagger to its other hand and slashed upward at Kit's thigh.

Searing pain burned his leg, and Kit dropped to his knee, clawing at the dagger stuck in his leg. His sudden movement caused the bragûl's hand to slip off the hilt, and Kit grabbed it. Holding his breath against the pain he knew would come, Kit yanked the dagger out of his thigh and buried it in the bragûl's chest.

Black blood spattered his hands and trickled down his wrists, but he had no time to be horrified. Clutching at his wounded leg, he staggered to his feet and raised his sword. Another bragûl turned to attack, but this time Kit was ready. He parried and lunged, matching each swing of the bragûl's sword. With a scream of mingled pain and fear, Kit swept his sword straight across the bragûl's bony shoulders and lopped off its head.

As its head toppled to the ground with a sickening squelch, Kit saw her.

A woman stalked into the clearing, twirling a long dagger or short sword in her hand, surveying the Protectors with a sneer. Strings of her long wheat-coloured hair were woven into a cap of braids holding down the rest of her loose, wavy hair like a net. Her dark brown eyes met his, and Kit flinched at the steel edge to her gaze—the razor-sharp certainty in the depths of her cavernous pupils that they would die at her hands.

Transfixed by the woman's confident cruelty, Kit failed to notice the bragûl charging his side until long talons dug into his arm and jerked him into the path of a crooked blade. His attempted parry was too slow.

But Ekina's wasn't.

She cut off the bragûl's blade-wielding hand with her spear, then spun her spear to thrust it into its heart in one fluid movement. The bragûl released its grip on Kit's arm and keeled over.

Panting, Kit tried to thank Ekina, but a noise between a squeak and a moan came out instead.

Ekina winked. "You're welcome."

A shuddering gasp escaped her lips, and surprised fear painted her wide eyes before they glazed over.

Kit looked down at the blade protruding from Ekina's chest.

The blade withdrew, and Ekina crumpled to the ground, revealing her attacker.

The wheat-haired woman stood there holding the blade stained with Ekina's blood.

Leering at Kit.

It was his turn next.

Staggering backward, Kit bumped into a battling bragûl and Lantíe. A sword pommel whacked his head, and darkness eclipsed all hope.

Six

Crowded with scores of Lantíés milling about the colour-ful, patterned woven mats where merchants sat selling their wares, the marketplace on the lowest path bordering the beach was normally one of Nensola's favourite places to be. Idle chatter hummed in the air, Lantíés discussing the latest catch or gossiping about the latest intrigue at the palace with languid nonchalance. Friends greeted each other warmly, sampling the fresh food to-gether. News of joy or grief was shared and celebrated or lamented together. Children played in the sand while their parents sold or purchased goods, watched but not hovered over. They chased each other, built structures of wet sand, splashed their toes in the surf, and butted antlers until a parent inevitably sighed and shouted, "Stop that before you poke someone's eye out!"

No one hurried. No one barked out pleas to buy their goods like Nensola had heard sellers did at other city markets. Craft could be appreciated and admired without the seller getting offended if it wasn't bought. What wasn't sold at market was traded in the city or up the coast in the small villages, or even as far as Carenthia when merchants traveled there by boat. She enjoyed the casual ambience of social community.

But today the drone of chatter buzzed in her ears like a relentless gnat. The shouts of children pounded in her head. Gulls screeched above them, wheeling in circles around the fish at market, waiting for their moment to swoop and snatch one. Pebbles dug into her legs and rear through the thin mat. She scowled at the browsers who strolled past her baskets of fish and newly woven nets without glancing at them. And her scowl deepened as she watched a little boy with deep green wings and no antlers try to fly and fail.

He stole a glance at her wings and paused, probably hoping for a smile of encouragement, an affirmation that he could fly if he only practised.

All she could offer him was an empty grimace.

He would not fly. With every generation, the magic in their wings dwindled. Her mother had been able to fly. Nensola could count the times she had flown on both her hands. Only a couple of children she had seen in Lothilya had wings, and she had never seen any of them fly. Soon most Lantian wings would be aesthetic only.

"If I didn't know better, I'd think Bren and Ninaya were playing a cruel joke on the Lantíes," her father commented beside her, seeing the direction of her gaze.

Nensola broke eye contact with the boy and stared at the mat's triangular pattern, pulling at a frayed thread.

"I know Ninaya can't control the molecular evolution of Air magic in the feathers, and I know Bren can't change the evolution of Earth creatures any more than I can catch the sun with my fishing net. Still, it does seem like we're continuing to be punished by *someone* for the sins of our peryton ancestors."

Ruffling her wings, Nensola said, "The Keepers don't care about us. They protect only the balance of Elemental magic and help the creatures of their element when it serves the equilibrium of that balance."

"It will be a sad day when Lantíes cease having wings," her father lamented, shaking his head.

Nensola shrugged. "I'm not so sure. If they lose their power to fly, what's the point of them? Why invite temptation for pirates to murder and steal and for other races to hide their bigotry behind a mask of fear?"

"You've got that all wrong, my friend," Kaliza interjected from behind her, coming to sit beside Nensola. She flipped her wavy chestnut hair over her bare tawny-skinned shoulder and pierced her friend's eyes with her periwinkle ones. "Your existence does not excuse bigotry or tempt malicious intent. Their desire to use you for their own ends reflects their vices, not yours."

Nensola's closest friend other than Kit had zero tolerance for small-minded ignorance and had always stood up for the rights of Lantíés, believing strongly in their worth to Carmelle and not trying to erase their past. Ironically, she had neither wings nor antlers.

Or maybe she tried so hard to protect Lantian traditions *because* she had only her pointed ears to mark her as Lantian.

"We can't control our evolution from perytons any more than the humans can control their evolution from apes," Kaliza continued, taking Nensola's silence as acclamation. "You don't see them wishing they could change their big mouths so we wouldn't be tempted to punch them."

"*Kaliza!*"

"What? Oh, come on! You can't tell me you have never wanted to punch a big mouth that spewed unsolicited hatred at you."

Nensola declined to comment.

"Speaking of humans with big mouths ..." Kaliza segued, leaving the hooked sentence hanging.

Nensola clamped her lips together, refusing to take the bait.

"Have you heard from Kit lately?"

"No."

"Don't tell me that boy finally gave up on you."

"I'm not usually that lucky."

"Maybe he's off pillaging the neighbouring village," her father suggested, his voice heavy with bitterness. He had not taken Kit's betrayal lightly.

"Actually, I heard he joined the Protectors," Vak'an, her father's friend, chimed in from the mat next to theirs, where he had obviously been eavesdropping. "Went on a bragûl raid with them a few days ago. Haven't seen him since."

Nensola's stomach clenched, hardening into a pit.

Lines creased her father's forehead. Lines of disgust at Kit's audacity, or worry?

"Where did you hear that, Vak'an?" her father asked his friend.

"From me," grunted a voice above them, and Nensola looked up to find Captain Harthlin approaching their mat, accompanied by his daughter, Aylí. She twisted her long copper hair in her bronzed fingers, eyes on the horizon instead of her companions.

When everyone met his announcement with a blank stare, he added, "Lord Eberon told me when I captained his vessel last night."

"But it can't be true," protested Nensola's father. "It doesn't make any sense. Why would Kit join the Protectors? What could he possibly have to gain?"

"I can think of something," muttered Kaliza, raising an eyebrow at Nensola.

"It is true, unfortunately."

A shadow stretched over their baskets, and Nensola looked up to see Captain Ní-brik looming over them, his thick antlers blocking out the sun. Ní-brik had been Setamíel's captain. Leaning heavily on a twisted driftwood cane, he shuffled his feet, wincing through fresh scars as his knee buckled a little. Guilt roiled in Nensola's gut at the satisfaction swelling in her chest upon seeing he had not escaped the bragûl unscathed when so many of his warriors had died.

"He came to me a few weeks ago, asking if he could join the Protectors. I trained him as best I could, but the bragûl were ... overwhelming. And with *her* there ... I didn't see a body, so I can't say for sure, but ... he is missing." Captain Ní-brik's sigh bore the weight of crushing too many Lantian hopes recently. Being the harbinger of tragedy must take its toll. "Presumed dead."

Blood rushed to Nensola's ears.

Kaliza gasped, but her father growled, "Well, dying to protect Lothilya was more than that pirate deserved."

Her stomach hollowed, the hard pit carved out as if she were a gutted fruit, leaving behind a yawning, gaping hole. She saw nothing through the dizzy spots and tears blurring her vision. No path forward. No hope.

Hugging her stomach, she lurched to her feet and fled.

The voices in her head drowned out the voices of her friends and family calling after her.

With each crashing wave, a story drowned her.

The swell of a wave roared.

An agonized sob mourned the loss of a friend in battle.

The rushing crescendo of cresting water rumbled.

A shriek of terror was cut short by a lightning strike.

The pummeling splash of the furled wave slamming into the sea thundered.

A mother's desperate cry pleaded for mercy.

Her mother's cry.

Tears streamed down Nensola's cheeks, sobs racking her chest.

The rolling *whoosh* of the wave's dying charge up the sand groaned, then faded with the receding surf.

Kit's strangled yell at the dagger in his leg weakened to a moan, blood pooling around him.

Death and despair flooded her mind, rushing in her ears, choking her lungs.

Her mother. Kit.

She screamed against the tightness in her chest, gasping at the relentless ache.

Seizing fistfuls of beach grass and digging her toes into the sand, she tried to anchor her body. Make it focus on something tangible outside her mind. She had come to the ocean instead of the river to force herself to confront the voices. Control them.

But the voices pulled her under.

Pushing her down to the black shadow that stalked her soul.

A shadow with wings and antlers. Like a peryton, homing in on its prey, biding its time until she was vulnerable enough to strike. To consume her like a human soul. To use her as a vessel to consume others.

Squeezing her eyes shut, she tried to squeeze the shadow out, barricade it from her heart.

But it lived within her. She could not deny the shadow's call any more than she could deny her lungs air to breathe.

Why did she fight it?

Maybe people's worst fears about her were well founded. Maybe the cacophony of voices in her head meant madness, not special talent. Maybe her peryton instincts were too strong to relinquish. Maybe she could only ever be defined by the past.

Too weak to rise above her grief and control the voices in her head without her mother's Water magic tricks to help. Too bloodthirsty to quell her vengeful thoughts. Too full of hate to feel hope.

A monster.

It was time to stop denying who she was.

Upon opening her eyes, she fixed them on the blood-red sun staining the horizon and embraced her soul's shadow.

The voices vanished. But in their place, a ravenous darkness burned through her veins, igniting an insatiable hunger for blood and vengeance.

Vengeance on the people who made her feel lesser.

On the pirates who had murdered her mother.

On the woman who had killed Setamíel.

On the bragûl who had killed Kit.

Rising to her feet, she unsheathed the dagger at her hip, and she took a few steps toward the village.

Her mother's voice rose above the blood pounding in her ears, a whispered echo rolling in with the waves as it had seven years ago.

Hope.

Nensola paused, shaking her mother's voice from her mind as though shaking her snagged antlers free from a branch. The shadow surged and swelled inside her, smudging out any spark of hope.

But her mother's voice rose again, this time as a story—a memory recalled from the past, sliding past the shadow with an image so strong it lit the darkness.

Her mother sat behind her on the beach, wings shielding them from the strong ocean breeze, braiding her hair. Eight-year-old Nensola built a house of sticks and shells in the sand.

Shadows blurred the edges of the image, black tendrils snaking toward her mother, but Nensola halted their progress, freezing them in place.

"Hope lives in us, Nen," her mother explained, pulling more strands of hair into the braid. "It ebbs and flows like the tide. Sometimes it is only a drip in the deepest, darkest caves of our hearts. Sometimes it overwhelms and consumes like a tidal wave. But it does not dry up. We can get lost in its maelstrom, but we cannot lose it."

"Then why do people feel despair?" Nensola asked.

"Because they have barred hope from their hearts. Built a wall to hold back its flow, because feeling hope in the face of sorrow is too painful. It's easier to believe hope has abandoned us. That it demanded too high a price. But hope demands no sacrifice. It simply asks to be let in."

A tear dripped off Nensola's chin.

Somewhere deep in the caverns of her heart, a tiny droplet of hope beaded and dripped.

The shadows tried to advance, to blot out the memory of her mother.

But she wouldn't let them.

She was tired of feeling useless, tired of her Storytelling gift building prison bars instead of opening vistas of freedom. She wasn't a vessel to be used. Voices of the past couldn't control her, and neither could the shadows of her ancestors.

Cupping that precious drop of hope, she buoyed it with stories. Stories of hope made from warm, positive memories. Her mother playing with her in the surf, splashing Nensola's wings and then taking flight with her own, hovering teasingly out of the reach of Nensola's splash. Dancing with her mother and Setamíel, laughing when her father joined in and immediately tangled his antlers in a low-hanging branch. Sampling food at the market with her sister. Hauling in nets overflowing with fish with her father. Kissing Kit in the moonlight.

The drop of hope grew, pooling into a lake.

Concentrating on pushing back the black tendrils of shadow, she willed them to recede.

Slowly they obeyed.

She drowned them in hope's tsunami.

The voices came rushing back, but Nensola softened them. Quieting their clamouring, soothing their desperation. Weeding out the extraneous and planting a few in the back of her mind.

Tears blurred Nensola's vision, but tears of joy didn't stain. She laughed, a light, giddy giggle of unbridled relief. Her shoulders relaxed, and her chest ballooned with possibility.

She was weightless.

Heart racing, she spread her wings—and pumped them as hard as she could.

Her feet lifted off the ground.

Laughter bubbled up from her chest and spilled out of her mouth. She released a euphoric cry and pumped her wings faster. Rising, climbing into the sky, leaving behind fear as the wind funneled through her antlers and unfurled her hair like a banner.

A banner declaring she would no longer hide. No longer deny the strengths of her past.

Swooping over the ruby-dappled ocean, she wheeled around and flew toward home.

She needed a word with her father.

When she reached her home, she found her father standing outside, his face lit by torchlight, gaping at her flying toward him.

Nensola buffeted the leaves like a gale with her powerful wing pumps to slow herself down, and she landed a few feet away from her father.

"We need to talk," she said without preamble, folding her wings behind her as she closed the gap between them. "You're wrong about Kit."

"What are you talking about? And how did you fly? You haven't flown in years."

"Hatred and despair have been weighing me down. But no more." Nensola clasped her father's hands in her own. "We have all been holding on to hate too long. Hate for the pirates that killed Mom. For the people who insist there's something to fear about Lantíés. Something that makes us different. Soulless. But Mom taught us all to believe in hope. For all Setamíel's strengths, she could never find hope. I don't want that to be me. And I don't want that for you."

Chin quivering, her father looked past her to the ocean. He clenched his jaw against the threat of tears. "The roots of hate are hard to dig up."

"Yes," Nensola agreed. "But if we don't try, the hate won't just grow. It will consume."

Taking a deep, shuddering breath, her father nodded. "But what does that have to do with Kit?"

"Don't you see, Father? We painted him with the same brush other races paint Lantíés with. They assume the worst about us, that all Lantié must have blackened hearts and a dormant desire to kill. All they see is the label of peryton. If we can't look past the label of pirate and see the person inside, then we're no better than our enemies. Hatred blinded me too. But we *know* Kit. We *know* the good person he is. A year of kindness should not be undone by a label. Kit always said we should embrace all of who we are, the good and the bad. I wasn't brave enough to face the bad before. But I am now. And I know in my heart what I need to do."

Touching her forehead to his, she inhaled deeply in unison with him, syncing their breaths, and their hearts.

Then she released her father's hands and took a step back.

Eyes bulging in alarm, her father matched her step and held out a halting hand, exclaiming, "Wait! What do you need to do?"

"Kit risked his life to help us," Nensola said, her gentle tone mirroring her slow, continued retreat. "To show us what we should have seen all along. He may be dead. But he may not be. There's still hope. I'm not going to let him die when there's a chance we can save him. And I'm not going to let my home and my people be destroyed."

Pride shone through the glistening tears in her father's eyes.

"I'm coming with you," he said.

Nensola beamed, a smile brighter than the stars.

"I hoped you would say that."

She held out her hand, extending the warmth of hope to her father.

Hope was like the sun on the ocean. It wasn't a tangible thing you could grasp, nor an emotion you could hold on to like love or hate. It was as elusive as a reflection, a glimmer of the light inside a person, refracting without breaking.

Its strength and endurance made hope a greater weapon than any their enemy had.

And Nensola planned to wield it against them.

Seven

S oaring low over the city, Nensola banked across ebony cliffs and glided over obsidian roofs, singing a song of hope. The words dripped with power, the images flashing through her mind clearer and more vibrant than any she had recalled before. This song was different. A call to community. A rally for change. A battle cry to defend the people. The epitome of hope.

She sang of wizards humbly asking the Lantíés for help, and lamps flickered on in windows below.

She sang of the Lantíés approaching Carenthia and Dharmaelia, seeing the cities besieged by the innumerable servants of Vashi crushing the mortal human race, some of whom refused to consort with the Lantíés, and their resolve to help save them.

Lantíés peered out into the night, scanning the skies for the source of the song and spotting Nensola wheeling above. The bright silver-white moon illuminated the constellations of awe in their eyes.

She sang of Lantíés standing hand in hand with humans, antlers brushing against helmets, wings and shields raised together, united against a common foe.

And slowly, leaving the comfort of their homes and venturing down the paths between houses, a few of the Lantíés followed her. And then a few more. Meeting at the crossroads, joining together in bands, hardened determination growing in the glint of their eyes and hard lines of their lips, they became a group.

After turning sharply over a bed of luminous algae, Nensola alighted smoothly at the foot of a bridge connecting the rocky peninsula dwellings to the forest dwellings of Lothilya. The stone bridge arced high over a group of small geysers, erupting occasionally from vents in the rock. Her father leaned his elbow upon the bridge's balustrade, waiting for her.

"How did it go?" he asked.

"They're coming."

A few minutes later, the group of Lantíés who had followed her song crested the ridge and halted before Nensola, waiting to hear why they should go any further.

Palms slick with sweat, Nensola glanced at her father's slackened jaw and unblinking eyes and wet her lips. Inspiring words came easy to her as a Storyteller. But wings flapped in her stomach instead of on her back at the thought of finding the right words without her gift. She wasn't a leader. Impassioned speeches were Kaliza's territory, or Setamíel's, not hers.

"We need to help the Protectors against this bragûl threat," Nensola began, quiet voice quivering. She clutched the hilt of her dagger to stop her fingers from shaking. "Our people are dying. Our enemy is multiplying. And the Protectors can't face them alone. We are a powerful people. We know what it is to face hate and rise above it. Why do we allow terror to continue?"

Murmurs rumbled through the group, and a few heads nodded their assent.

Confidence steadied Nensola's voice, which grew louder with each word. "The Protectors need our help. We are stronger united. Let's show them our resilience. Let's fight not only to protect our land, but to protect our people!"

Her father's shining eyes lent her strength.

"Who will take a stand with me?" she shouted, jutting her chin up in defiance.

And to her surprise, they cheered. Every one of them. Raising fists in the air and tossing their magnificent antlers, they surged over the bridge, following Nensola into the forest.

Taking up her song again, Nensola guided them down the path, letting the luminous plants carpeting the forest floor and the glowing silver sap snaking around the birch and aspen trees light their way. When they passed the forest homes nestled between giant roots or among the lower, thick branches of the trees, the Lantíes following her started peeling off, racing to knock on doors and spread the message to their friends and families. More Lothilyans joined their group as they walked, swelling their ranks until they spilled off the path and had to wend through the trees.

"What is all this?" Captain Ní-brik shouted, running to catch up with them.

"We're going to find Kit and claim back our land from the bragûl," Nensola answered, pausing her song. "Show them that we stand united and will not back down. We may not have a proper army, but we have heart, and a fierce love for our people."

"Nensola … I know you're grieving," said Captain Ní-brik with placating patience. "I know Setamíel's and Kit's deaths must be unbearable—"

"We don't know Kit is dead," interrupted Nensola. "He's just missing."

"Yes, I know I said that, but … the bragûl won't just let him live. Why would they take prisoners? They're soulless monsters without mercy."

"People think *we* are soulless monsters too," said Nensola quietly.

"Are you trying to say there's good in the bragûl? They're Vashi's minions, bred for one purpose."

"Of course she's not saying that," her father chimed in from beside her.

"No, I'm not saying they're good," agreed Nensola. "But we are forgetting about the woman leading these bragûl. We don't know what her reason is for attacking Lothilya yet. Maybe it would be to her advantage to keep prisoners."

Nensola refrained from voicing her fear of what the woman would *do* with prisoners.

"Maybe you're right, and she would take prisoners," Captain Ní-brik conceded. "But you can't just gather a group of civilians to fight a battle on behalf of the kingdom. There are rules that need to be followed. Rules established by Lord Eberon and Lady Leilaní. You need their permission, their blessing, their *resources*. Where are your weapons, your armour?"

"Perhaps you could help us with that, Captain Ní-brik," came Kaliza's voice from behind Nensola, and she turned to see her friend hurrying through the crowd toward her. A cloth-wrapped bundle teetered in her arms, and she unrolled it at Nensola's feet to reveal a pile of swords, daggers, bows, and quivers full of arrows. "I can only carry so much."

Nensola beamed at her friend, tears beading in the corners of her eyes.

Clasping Nensola's forearms, Kaliza touched her forehead to her childhood friend's.

"Your song is beautiful, Nen," she breathed. Her voice broke as she added, "You *flew*."

Nensola barked a raspy laugh, wiping her tears with her wing. "Thank you for coming."

Captain Ní-brik still had another objection. "The Protectors have been trying to stop these bragûl attacks. No offence, but what makes you think a band of untrained civilians will succeed where trained and skilled warriors have not?"

Nensola felt the eyes of every Lantíé within hearing boring into her head.

"I don't know that we will succeed," Nensola admitted. "And maybe all I will gain here is a cell in the lord and lady's palace. But there is strength in numbers, and in hope. The bragûl expect trained soldiers. But an overwhelming surge of sudden hope may turn the tide and banish the shadows."

A rustling wave rippled through the crowd as feet shifted and stirred. But no one left.

Captain Ní-brik heaved a reluctant sigh. "Well, if I can't stop you, I guess I will join you. I *and* the Protectors."

The crowd erupted in cheers.

Nensola threw her arms around the captain, whispering, "Thank you."

"Keep marching east along this path," Captain Ní-brik instructed when they broke apart. "I'll meet you where the path ends near Lothilya's borders."

Facing the line of shadowy bragûl brandishing their crooked weapons and baring their sharp fangs, Nensola had to admit the wave of hope swelling in her heart deflated a little. Even with all the Protectors and the band of civilians she had mustered, the bragûl's numbers still looked insurmountable. Her bow shrank to a stick. The light arrows rattled like pebbles in the quiver girded at her waist instead of slung across her back, because of her wings.

When Captain Ní-brik had rejoined Nensola with a contingent of Protectors, each carrying a few extra weapons, and asked her which one she would like, she had chosen the bow. Setamíel had taught her how to shoot, knowing it was a weapon good for both fighting and hunting, should Nensola ever need to do either. Setamíel had always tried to proactively counteract the negative what-ifs. What if she died in battle one day? What if their father never returned home from a fishing trip? How would her sister fend for herself? Nensola had often complained of the lessons being unnecessary, but she was grateful for them now. At the encouragement of the Protectors, many civilians had also chosen bows or spears, weapons that might allow them to distance themselves from the heart of the fray and avoid engaging in more skilled hand-to-hand combat.

Her companions' shallow, uneven breathing reverberated in Nensola's ears as if she were underwater.

Had she led them all to their deaths?

To her left, Captain Ní-brik unsheathed his sword, ready, despite his limp, for another fight. To her right, her father shifted a spear from hand to hand. His watery eyes glinted with determination, and Nensola suspected he thought of Setamíel. Chancing a glance at Kaliza behind her, she rolled her eyes at her friend's grin.

Though the bragûl clogged the spaces between trees ahead of them, Nensola saw no woman among them.

And no Kit.

Ignoring her sinking heart, she pulled an arrow from her quiver.

Whatever fate awaited them today, it wouldn't change by waiting.

She fit an arrow to the string, aimed it at a bragûl, and released it.

It sank into the darkness between its red eyes.

With a chorus of high-pitched, grating shrieks, the bragûl charged, black streaks of shadow streaming behind them.

Captain Ní-brik raised his fist and shouted, "Hold your ground! Loose arrows on my signal!"

After a few seconds, Ní-brik uncurled his fist.

Arrows streaked into the bragûl's midst, toppling bodies. Ní-brik closed his fist again, and the Lantíes nocked more arrows. When the bragûl were halfway to them, Ní-brik opened his fist.

More bodies fell beneath the barrage of arrows, but not enough. The bragûl broke upon them like a wave.

The Protectors charged to meet them, swinging their swords in graceful arcs or cutting, dodging, and parrying attacks with practised skill. Surging forward with the Lantíé, Nensola loosed arrows as fast as she could nock them, chest swelling a little with pride when they hit bragûl more often than tree trunks or the ground.

Nensola and some of the other civilians circled around the edges of the fray, loosing arrows at bragûl. A few bragûl charged the outliers, and when they got too close to loose arrows, Nensola drew her dagger. She screamed as a blade drew across her arm, and she leapt into the air, beating her wings to hover just out of the bragûl's reach. She fit an arrow to the string of her bow and buried it in the bragûl's heart, spilling its black blood.

Nensola swooped low to grab an armful of large rocks and hefted them into the air. Flying closer to the trees the bragûl had emerged from, she pelted them with the rocks, watching with satisfaction as their bodies crumpled when the stones connected with their heads.

A small figure at the base of a tree behind the horde of bragûl caught her eye. Peering closer, she realized it squirmed against the ropes binding it to the tree, struggling to break free.

A figure with curls of clove-coloured hair mixed with congealed blood matted to his forehead. Heartbeat stuttering alongside lungs suddenly bereft of breath, Nensola froze, forgetting to flap her wings.

Kit.

She plummeted to the ground.

Extending her wings out at the last second, Nensola slowed her fall enough to topple from buckled knees instead of slamming into the ground, and tuck into a roll. Winded and aching all over, she heaved her battered and bruised body up and turned to face Kit.

Their eyes locked. Kit's wide with awe and yearning. Nensola's brimming with tears.

"Nensola," he breathed, elongating the letters as though savouring them on his tongue. "You came for me."

"I'm so sorry, Kit," cried Nensola, rushing to cut his bonds with her dagger.

"I was supposed to apologize first."

"I was wrong to judge you so quickly when I found out you were a pirate. I just panicked. Pirates killed my mom, and I let hatred consume me."

Kit's face paled. "I'm so sorry. I wondered if it was something like that, but I couldn't get near enough to ask you."

"I know. I'm sorry."

"No. I'm sorry that I kept that from you. I just wanted to break free from past labels and start fresh, but—"

"It's *all right*, Kit. I get it," Nensola assured him, cutting the last of his bonds. She kissed him before he could apologize again, swift but sure, lingering with the promise of the words she didn't have time to say. "Come on, let's get you out of here."

But Kit reached for her face, turned it back to his own, and captured her lips in another kiss. Deeper, reluctant to let her go again. "You saved me," he murmured against her lips, and she knew he meant in more ways than rescuing him from the bragûl.

"Well, not quite yet," crowed a voice from behind Nensola. Kit froze in her arms, fearful eyes fixated on a spot over her shoulder. Slowly Nensola turned around, one hand still holding Kit's.

A woman with hair like thatched wheat sneered at their display of affection.

The woman who had killed her sister.

Nensola gripped Kit's hand tighter to stop herself from clawing the arrogant sneer off her face.

"How quick you are to accept the flaws of a human. If only humans would extend Lantíés the same courtesy."

"Kit *does* extend me the same courtesy."

"A noble pirate, is he? A rare breed indeed. I wonder how long that nobility will dampen his desire to steal. To seize the opportunity for personal gain, no matter the cost. To steal, for example, those admirable wings with the Air magic still intact."

"I would never," growled Kit, his voice low in warning.

"Yes, love is always enough to overcome our flaws. Until it isn't. Maybe your love would prove strong enough. But would hers? Stolen glances of love would turn suspicious. 'Is he admiring my face, or my wings?' Suspicion would trigger the shadows in her soul, and doubt would taint every interaction with thoughts of vengeance."

"How do you know so much about us?" challenged Nensola.

"Oh, I was eavesdropping," the woman admitted, pointing between herself and the tree behind her. "I'm afraid it's rather a bad habit of mine. People say all sorts of fascinating things before they die. It's why I kept you alive. As soon as I saw a human fighting alongside Lantíés, I knew there must be a story there. I wanted to hear it."

Nensola gaped at this woman who spoke so unabashedly about her evil deeds without reservation. "Who *are* you?"

"Rashad."

The name raised the hairs on Nensola's arms, though she couldn't quite place it. Scanning the trees behind Rashad, Nensola observed the battle raging on but couldn't tell if her father still fought in it. She forced her gaze to return to Rashad and swallowed past the grating dryness in her throat.

"What do you want with Lothilya?" Nensola demanded.

"Me? Nothing at all! What my master wants, however ..." Rashad spread her arms wide in a vague gesture that suggested both everything and nothing. "But the real question is what you want. You're here now, in the middle of a battle, with the perfect opportunity to exact your revenge and make it look like a casualty of war. Deep down, your peryton roots fester. Clamouring for the blood of your enemies, the pirates who killed your mother. Embrace the shadow, and I will help you claim your soul."

Kit stroked the curve between her thumb and forefinger but didn't dismiss Rashad's offer with a derisive guffaw or beg for mercy. He just waited for Nensola's answer.

In the distance, Nensola finally spotted her father. A bragûl slashed at his antlers and severed several tines with one stroke. Gasping, Nensola shut her eyes against the darkness creeping back into her soul. The black shadows worming tendrils into her heart. Her boiling blood screamed for vengeance.

Squeezing Kit's hand, she concentrated on the stream of hope trickling in her heart and thought of her sister daring to hope she could assume the mantle of mother and protector at thirteen. She thought of Kit's hope for a new life, a place to call home. And she thought of her mother's unwavering belief that hope could be found even in the darkest moments. Feeding these thoughts to her own stream of hope, she coaxed it into a rushing river. A wall of waves. A towering tidal wave that obliterated the shadows.

"I will not kill Kit. I will never forget my mother, but I don't need to avenge her. Vengeance consumed me once. I won't let it consume me again."

"Not even to kill me and avenge your sister?"

Rashad smirked, a twisted hunger hooking her mouth and glinting in her eyes.

"Not even then," said Nensola, her voice quiet but firm. Steady. Finite.

Rashad's smirk soured. "Then it's time for your story to end."

Nensola handed Kit her dagger and drew her bow.

But Rashad did not attack with weapons of steel.

Kit's dagger dropped from his limp hand, and a fountain of water spouted beneath him, shooting him into the sky.

Magic.

Shouting hoarsely, Kit flailed atop the water, searching desperately for something to hold onto—but the water vanished.

He plunged down. A scream ripped from his lips as he dropped.

Nensola launched herself into the air and streaked toward him, arms outstretched. When she caught him under his arms, she dropped like a rock with the sudden extra weight but managed to flap her wings hard enough to stop their descent a few feet from the ground.

Thinking only of putting as much distance as possible between them and Rashad, Nensola tried to fly away, but her wings weighed her down. She inched toward the ground, the strength in her wings fading.

At first she thought Rashad must be turning her wings to stone. But solidifying shouldn't feel like leaking. Something drained from her feathers. Weakening her wings. Dragging her down to the ground. Kit slipped from her grasp, but his toes had already brushed the grass. He landed on his feet. Nensola landed beside him.

With a strangled cry of horror, Nensola tried desperately to raise her body off the ground.

But she couldn't fly.

The Air magic was being siphoned from her feathers.

Tears burned her eyes, blurring her vision, sucking the moisture from her mouth.

Rashad was stealing the magic in her feathers, like the pirates had stolen her mother's.

A painful lump constricted her throat. She tried to wheeze breaths past it, but no air escaped her deflated lungs.

Her feathers started moulting. Twirling to the ground like seeds from a maple tree. Littering the grass with fragments of violet and bronze.

Hope slipped through her fingers like cupped water.

But she did not let it drain.

Rashad cried out in pain. Her hold on Nensola broke.

Nensola's feathers ceased draining. She collapsed, crumpling to her knees.

Through the translucent sheen of her tears, she saw the arrow impaled right through Rashad's hand. Lantíes surrounded them, forming a circle. The cold glint of nocked arrows and hefted spears flashed at Rashad from every angle. No bragûl pursued them.

"Leave them alone!" Nensola's father commanded from somewhere in the circle.

Rashad hesitated, maybe assessing her chances against the Lantíes surrounding her.

"This isn't the end. I'll be back, with greater numbers. And you will beg for death."

Arrows flew from all sides, but Rashad vanished.

Hunched over her moulted violet-tipped bronze feathers, strewn across the ground, Nensola ran them through her fingers and wept. She didn't bottle her sorrow. She let the sobs rack her body while Kit stroked her back between her wings.

She had lost some of her flying feathers.

The enemy had not yet been vanquished.

But she had held on to hope.

And the hope of a united people protecting their home remained strong.

Eight

Sitting on the sand with his elbows propped on his drawn-up knees, Kit fiddled with his father's longitude device, steeped in memories of Earth. His father chiding him for trying to eat the grapes he picked to make wine. His mother pinning him tightly to her side when they walked down the streets of Gibraltar with Captain Firth, shielding him from the hurt, hateful glares of their people. Captain Firth standing with him at the prow of their ship, laughing and tousling Kit's hair after teasing him about looking for mermaids.

Though he carried these memories with him everywhere, they belonged to a different Kit—a Kit too afraid to be more than half of himself at a time.

He wasn't afraid anymore.

Beside him, Nensola sorted through shells and sea gems.

"What's the criteria for being worthy of Setamíel?" Kit asked, raising an eyebrow at a rather ordinary-looking brown stone Nensola had just added to the keep pile.

"They can't just be pretty," Nensola explained. "They must have specific meaning to Setamíel. Something that matches her looks, like this brown stone the exact colour of her antlers. Or something that reflects her personality, like this shell armoured with barnacles on the outside but a soft lilac on the inside."

Kit recognized the resemblance immediately and smiled, leaning over to plant a kiss on Nensola's temple. "You're right. That shell is *exactly* her."

Nensola snuggled into his side and continued sorting.

It had been two days. Two days since Nensola had rescued him from Rashad's clutches. Two days since they had been reunited in forgiveness.

Two days since he had felt whole again.

Captain Ní-brik had found Setamíel's body after Rashad and the bragûl had vanished. The bragûl had dragged a pile of fallen Lantian bodies into an encampment they had set up not too far from where the latest battle had taken place. Kit's skin crawled thinking about what they had planned to do with those bodies.

Tomorrow they honoured Setamíel's life with the traditional death ceremony specific to Lantíés of Lothilya.

But today ... today was theirs.

"How are your wings?" Kit ventured gently.

Nensola shrugged, the sagging lines of her crestfallen face belying her feigned nonchalance. "Lady Leilaní said Rashad failed to drain all the magic. I ... I may never be able to fly to the same heights as before, but ... Lady Leilaní thinks that with time and her magic, she can restore enough Air magic to the feathers that I should be able to feel wind in my hair again as I soar over Lothilya."

Kit's chest ached and lightened simultaneously. "I hate that Rashad has taken away your ability to fly as freely as your ancestors, like you deserve."

"Getting what you deserve is a rare occurrence. I'm just happy to have the hope of flying again. My mom didn't get that chance," Nensola added, her voice small. "The pirates came for the Air magic that resides at the molecular level in our feathers. The magic loses its potency once severed from its life source, but even a little bottled magic is worth a lot. My mother tried to defend herself with the little Water magic she possessed, but it was never much, and it could not save her."

"I do understand why it was so hard for you to accept piracy as just one aspect of who I am. I didn't tell you because it was easier to avoid it than accept it. I didn't like feeling so lost all the time. I used to resent my mother," Kit admitted, his words bloated with bitterness, swelling his throat. "I thought she was selfish for choosing to remarry instead of staying true to her people, and my father's memory. For fractioning my heart, dividing it between cultures and loved ones. But I know now how brave she was for daring to hope amid so much loss. She recognized people for their potential and saw past their labels. She saw my stepfather's heart and chose not to paint him with the same brush as the British who had killed my dad. And even when they shunned her, she still took fierce pride in her people, knowing their hearts were not all the same either. She always looked at the individual, not the group."

"I would have liked to meet your mother," mused Nensola, pausing her sorting to gaze out at the slate-grey ocean reflecting overcast skies.

"She would have loved you," Kit insisted, laughing.

Nensola turned to face Kit, eyes shining with tears. "Really?"

"From the day we met, you have led with hope. You extended a greeting to me and opened your heart and mind to the possibilities that come with acceptance. You never asked me to be more than who I was. I love you, Nensola," said Kit ardently, stomach fluttering in time with his stuttering heart. "And I want to stay in Arwé with you, if that's what you want."

Nensola took his hands, her gaze steady and sure as she looked deep into his eyes. "I love you too, Kit. And of course I want you to stay."

Kit smiled against her lips.

His anchor had finally found a place to take hold.

Trailing her fingers through the river behind her house, Nensola cupped a white nalalíté flower in the palm of her other hand. Since the battle with the bragûl and Rashad, Nensola had been thinking about what Setamíel had said the last time she had seen her. Maybe a small part of her *had* been clinging to the hope that her mother would return one day. But like people, not all hopes were the same. Hope could not change her life if it stopped her from living it.

It was time to let this hope go.

Nensola closed her eyes, letting memories of her mother flow through her like the river's current. She breathed deeply, weaving those memories into the fabric of her soul.

She lowered the flower and held it poised just above the water for a moment—then let go.

The nalalíté dipped and bobbed over the river's ripples, carried downstream, until it rounded a bend and vanished from sight.

Goodbye, Mom.

After the battle, her father had asked if Nensola would become a warrior now, like her sister, a half-smile sliding across his face as though he was unsure whether he asked in earnest or jest. But Nensola had replied without hesitation. She would use her gift to fight hate with the strongest weapon she had: stories of hope.

Fiery orange and vermilion stained the rows of cloudlets rippling across the sky and sparked in the droplets arcing over Nensola's hand from Kit's paddle behind her. His strong, steady strokes pulled their boat through the mercifully smooth ocean, leaving

Nensola free to study the deep golden glow kissing her sister's cheeks.

Setamíel lay on a woven *hibinco* mat upon an aspen-rod bier, her braids woven between her antlers in her favourite warrior style, arms by her side with her palms up to greet her ancestors, her Protector armour cleaned and polished. White nalalíté flowers encircled her body, dotted with shells and sea gems. The bier floated between Nensola's boat and her father's, held in place by both remaining members of Setamíel's family.

A dozen or so more boats accompanied them, friends and family who wished to celebrate Setamíel's life. After rounding the tip of the peninsula on the southern side, they followed the line of the coast, hugging its craggy curves in places and paddling further out where the waves were too rough for Setamíel's bier. Gliding past an outcropping of jumbled rocks flung into the ocean like a reaching arm, Nensola spotted an island entirely populated with aspen trees.

"Is that Aspengrove Island?" Kit asked, a note of reverence in his voice.

"Yes," replied Nensola, watching the yellowing leaves flutter in an early autumn breeze. "That is the home of our peryton ancestors."

"It's beautiful," Kit said simply.

Nensola reached back and squeezed his hand.

"Did you know the trees in a cluster of aspens are all connected?" she asked Kit. "They share one life source, connected through their roots. Separate, but always part of a whole. Growing, suffering, and thriving together. For all their flaws, perytons shared the same values as the aspens of their home, as do the Lantíés. Setamíel would be at peace knowing she could rest in a place of community."

Nensola could feel Kit's smile warming her back, a warmth that spread to her chest and elicited a deep sigh of contentment.

When they finally reached the island, the honey-drizzled horizon had been washed away by azure rivers. After grouping their boats closer together, they began a slow paddle around the island. Tradition dictated a dirge be sung as they paddled, but Nensola recalled the story of Setamíel's life instead.

She sang of Setamíel's weightless childhood. Her carefree seaside antics, the games they played with their mother. The possibility dangling from every star.

She sang of the demise of Setamíel's innocence. The bitter hate that had replaced hope when she had shouldered the weight of her family's well-being. The questioned intentions, the impatience for the impractical, the dismissal of dreams as naive idealism.

But through the triumphs and tribulations of Setamíel's life, Nensola wove a common thread of hope—a hope that still prevailed in her sister's life despite her disdain for the concept. Hope that their family would be all right after their mother died had elicited a desire to care for them. Hope had driven her to protect them against further danger. Hope had instilled in her the belief that life after loss was still worth living and protecting. She had held hope for the people she had loved most. Hope her father could carry on after losing his wife. Hope her sister could control her gift without their mother and learn to embrace it.

Setamíel's song was a ballad of hate and hope.

Aspen leaves fluttered and shivered in the breeze, dancing to Nensola's song in tune with the twinkling stars dusting the deepening sky. When they had completed their circle around the island and Nensola had sung her song, they pulled the bier up onto the island's shore, raising it onto an ancient azure lapis platform.

Nensola reached into her dress pocket and pulled out a handful of her violet-tipped bronze feathers and placed them on her sister's chest. She knew their Air magic had been depleted, but she hoped they might help her sister's soul take flight to the stars.

After pricking his thumb, her father bent low and pressed his warm Lantian blood to an indent in the lapis stone, igniting its fluorescence. The crystals of deep blue lazurite within caught the starlight.

Nensola reached for Kit's hand, and they waited.

When deep blue skies blackened to midnight and the stars shone their brightest, Setamíel's body glowed a paler blue than the lapis, and tiny blue spots of light lifted from her chest. Floating through the air, they swirled higher, illuminating the aspens as they rose above the island and danced among the stars.

Tears streamed silently down Nensola's cheeks.

They stood there, breathing deeply, eyes tracing the constellations, until the stars faded, and the lightening sky revealed a cool grey mist hovering around the shores of a cerulean sea.

Nensola helped wrap Setamíel's body in weighted cloth, and with the first dusty rose light of dawn, they lowered her into the ocean. Returning her body to Arwé so new life may be created.

Because hope didn't always mean winning. Sometimes it meant holding space for the triumphs of loved ones. A community. A nation. Nensola understood now what her mother had always tried to teach her. Hope meant never giving up, despite everything she'd lost, holding on to even just one droplet. Because when it fell, it would always have a ripple effect.

And all it took was a ripple to change the world.

Author's Note

Thank you for reading *A Ballad of Hate and Hope*. If this is your first immersion into the world of Arwé, I hope it has inspired you to read the rest of the series. If you read this after already reading *A Spark From Embers*, I hope it added to your understanding of Arwé, and enhanced your reading experience of the series.

I know time is precious and leaving reviews can be daunting, but I would be ever so grateful and honoured if you would consider leaving a review on Goodreads or Amazon. Other than purchasing a book, leaving a review or rating helps support an author, and will help other readers find the book and decide whether they want to read it. And I of course value and appreciate your feedback.

If you are reading this book through my newsletter, thank you so much for subscribing! You can look forward to exclusive access to future novellas soon. If you purchased a paperback copy of this book and are not yet subscribed to my newsletter, I encourage you to consider subscribing through my website at www.kayleaprime. com. Through my newsletter, you will be privy to monthly writing updates, first announcements about upcoming books and cover reveals, ARC opportunities, and other exclusive content. Maybe I'll even throw you a deleted scene or secret snippet once in a while.

You can also find me across most social media platforms under the handle @kayleaprime.

Thank you again for your support!

-Kaylea Prime

Acknowledgements

A Ballad of Hate and Hope came together quickly, a tidal wave idea that swept me away and created a ripple effect with the force of its energy. Those ripples touched a lot of people, and I am indebted to them for their help and support in making this story a reality.

Naturally, those first ripples touched my family. My husband Sid, who read my outline, fact-checked my research, and became one of my alpha readers. Who helped with all the technical, background details of publishing a book. Who supported me with endless patience, writing fuel (snacks, tea & encouragement) to get me through the nights I wrote until 3am, and feedback on my story. Your love and support is invaluable.

Jade and Eralyn, for being my light in dark places. My droplet of hope I cling to, the hope that creates waves of joy. Your smiles and words of encouragement light up my life and inspire me, and I'm honoured by your unconditional love and faith in your mother's writing dreams. Thank you for your patience and indulgence, even on the days when I have to dedicate more time to writing to meet a deadline.

My parents Sylvia and Ron, and my sisters Candace and Tamara, for their words of encouragement and support in promoting this story. You have been there every step of the way on my writing journey with me, and I cannot express how much your unwavering love and support mean to me.

My amazing critique partner, friend, and alpha reader Bethany. You carved out time in your busy life while trying to write your own stories to read this story and provide such thoughtful feedback and encouragement. You exchanged countless emails with me to make sure I succeeded in publishing my first novella. You dropped everything to help promote it at the most important times. I could not have done this without your support.

Thank you to my editor Leonora, who smoothed all my inconsistencies. Your attention to detail, especially when it came to historical references and anachronisms, was so appreciated, as was your efficiency on a tight deadline.

To everyone who has supported me at every stage of both the writing of *A Ballad of Hate and Hope* and my author journey as a whole, I thank you from the bottom of my heart. Every like, comment, and share on social media, every encouraging exclamation of support, every time you tell someone else about my story, has meant so much to me. You give me hope.

And of course, thank *you*, dear reader, for taking a chance on this whirlwind novella and choosing to spend time with my characters and stories. I can never thank you enough, and I hope it was worth your time.

About the Author

Kaylea Prime is the author of the fantasy series, *Tears of Flame*. She is also a librarian with a passion for planning epic programs that immerse kids and teens into their favourite literary worlds. When she's not writing or working as a librarian, she can be found exploring the beautiful wilderness around her home in Clearwater, British Columbia, with her two kids, husband, and two golden retrievers.

www.kayleaprime.com